Maya's Quest 2: A Search For Meaning
A novel by Wai Chan

Maya's Quest: A Search For Meaning

Maya's Quest, Volume 2

WAI CHAN

Published by Wai Chan, 2024.

MAYA'S QUEST: A SEARCH FOR MEANING

First edition. October 18, 2024.

ISBN: 979-8986811543

Written by WAI CHAN.

Table of Contents

Chapter One - First Flight

The *Phoenix* moved steadily along a hundred meters or so above the forested landscape, pushing farther west from Greensboro with each passing moment. The aerostat, consisting of a gasbag protected by impact-resistant plastic armor, was propelled by solar-powered engines with two small gas turbines for emergency backup. It was manned by a crew from what had once been the Micronesian nation of Palau.

Several of the islands had been in conflict with one another for generations following the Dark Years, but their differences had been put aside, largely due to the efforts of Maya Komarov, who was now in charge of this expedition to the "lost continent" of North America.

Maya leaned on the window sill, almost hypnotized by the treetops passing smoothly below. They were about two hundred and seventy kilometers from their base in Greensboro now, on an exploratory flight. The *Phoenix,* one of a small flotilla of similar ships currently exploring the continent for the first time in two centuries, had conducted several of these over the past few weeks, venturing south, north, and now west.

Maya tore her attention from the peaceful scene below the airship and put it back on her memex. She had been using the data pad to check the level of efficiency in the solar cells, which had been trending slightly downward beginning a day after they left Greensboro. The decline was aggravating in part because there seemed to be no reason for it, but also because it seemed to be increasing.

And that wasn't an encouraging development.

After a moment she got up from her seat and made her way forward to the cockpit, where her boyfriend, Jame Natwick, was in the co-pilot seat chatting with Priscilla Burns, the pilot.

"How's it going up here?" Maya asked as she squeezed into the little space, which was crammed with instruments.

Jame grinned at her. He had brown hair, a strong jaw and, in her opinion, gorgeous hazel eyes. "Hey, sweet," he said.

"Sweet yourself," she said fondly, tapping his shoulder. "Hellay, Cilla."

Burns, fortyish, fit, and buxom, nodded in acknowledgement but said nothing. Her eyes remained locked on the ship's instrument panel. Maya suppressed a sigh. For whatever reason, she and Cilla did not get along, never had. Some people had positive chemistry with each other, like she had with Jame. But with others the chemistry was neutral or, in the case of Priscilla Burns, negative. They could work together as colleagues, and had mutual respect, but Maya had long since given up the idea of ever being friends with the pilot.

And that was fine.

"Nothing showing up with the cells?" Jame asked. Though nominally an IT specialist, for which he had been assigned to this expedition, he was also an enthusiastic amateur airman, and often took the co-pilot's post—initially over Burns's objections, until he had proved to her satisfaction that he could handle the craft.

"Nothing," Maya replied. "We're either going to have to land and run a full diagnostic or keep going and hope for the best."

Priscilla scoffed. "There's no place to land here." She gestured at the landscape. An endless carpet of trees stretched out ahead, with a cliff or small mountain of to the southwest. "And I don't want to go back to Greensboro Base before we reach our turn-around point."

Jame exchanged glances with Maya and lifted one shoulder in a quick shrug.

"What concerns me more," the pilot went on, "is that line of clouds. Storms blow up pretty quick around here."

Maya looked through the windshield. Sure enough, dark clouds lay directly ahead to the west. She opened her mouth to say something but before she could an alarm buzzed, and a light flared red on the instrument panel.

"Bloody—" Burns began, but the ship lurched. Maya grabbed Jame's seat back for support.

"Starboard prop shaft seized up," Burns said through clenched teeth. "It never rains but it pours... no pun intended."

"Its armature is overheating," Jame said, scanning the meters. "I'm taking it offline." He flipped a couple of switches. The *Phoenix* began swinging to the right.

Burns wore. "Shut the other one down, too," she said. Otherwise we'll be going in circles. I'll fire up the turbines."

As she spoke a fork of lightning sprang out of the gathering darkness to the west.

Uh-oh, Maya thought. "Uh, should we be trying to avoid that?" she asked.

"You should go aft and tell everyone to strap in," Jame said.

She turned and left the cockpit to pass the message along to the other members of the expedition. "Storm ahead," she said, as she took her seat at her console and fastened her safety belt. "We're in for some turbulence."

"Oh, great," said Miron Whitley, raking a strand of his long red hair out of his face. He was a former student of Maya's from her days as a professor of astronomy at the University of Eil Malk, back on their home island. They had had clashes, but those conflicts, like the ones between the islands, had since been resolved, and she'd had no qualms about recommending him for this exploratory mission. He had been after all the most talented computer expert among her university students, and, as a result of a childhood spent largely boating on the waters around their island home, had a real love of and knack for navigation—which was his primary function on the aerostat.

And on this trip he had proved his worth more than once, validating her decision.

"Miron," she said mildly, "if you don't strap in, you may find yourself bouncing around the cabin."

"Yeah, yeah," he grumbled, but he secured his harness. "Say, where the devil *are* we, anyway?" He tapped at his memex. "Oh, okay; not far from someplace called Asheville, assuming there's anything left of it." There usually weren't much in the way of ruins in this region; the weather could be extreme, and the forest grew quickly enough that most signs of civilization had been obliterated in the years following the asteroid strike in 2173, nearly three centuries ago. That had been the result of a botched attempt to move the space rock into orbit around Earth. The impact had all but destroyed humanity. Some wealthy survivors had established city-buildings, bionispheres, on remote South Pacific islands, like Maya's home, Eil Malk. Now, hundreds of years later, men were exploring their ruined world, struggling to establish footholds on land that had been abandoned.

Maya called up a weather radar app on her memex and saw with dismay that they were flying right into the tempest. "People," she said, "I think we—"

She was interrupted by a blinding flare of lightning, close by, followed almost immediately by a crack of thunder that made her jump. Her first impulse was to head for the cockpit, but she knew that the people flying the *Phoenix* were going to be busy and needed to concentrate. They didn't need someone—her—kibitzing. So she stayed where she was and occupied herself with nervously tearing a tissue into small pieces.

The storm grew more intense. There didn't seem to be any way to fly around it or above it; the airship was struggling to maintain altitude as it was, thanks in part to the malfunctioning prop. In situations like this, the props were useful to maintain trim, even though the turbines provided more punch. Without them, the craft was less than nominally stable.

The other expedition members, buckled into their seats around her, conversed in low tones of stared, white-faced, out of the ports.

"I've lost contact with base," Miron said through gritted teeth.

"That can't be good," Maya said. "That's not good, right?"

"Well, no," he said, not bothering to hide the sarcasm in his tone. "I mean—" Another stupendous peal of thunder drowned out the rest of his sentence.

May felt sweat popping out on her forehead. Back home on Eil Malk, storms occasionally swept the island, but there everyone knew what to do, and the bionisphere was well protected. Here, they had only the fragile shielding of the airship's car between them and the fury of the storm.

She gripped the arms of her chair and did her best to slow her breathing. From the cockpit a message crackled over the PA system: "Downburst! Hang on!"

Miron turned to Maya, his face etched with anxiety. "What's a downburst?"

"They're strong downdrafts within thunderstorms," she replied. "So we could lose a thousand feet of altitude in a few second—" But the rest of her sentence was cut off when the aircraft dropped precipitously, causing all the people around her to cry out in alarm. Maya's stomach rebelled and she grabbed for a sick bag. Alarms blared, but she was too occupied with trying not to throw up on herself to care. The *Phoenix* lurched again and lost more altitude. More people yelled.

The ship swung sickeningly from side to side, and Maya heaved again. She *hated* vomiting. She tried to regain control of herself, but before she could there was a splintering crash. Something hit her head, and she blanked out.

HER RETURN TO AWARENESS came amid groans and wailing. She seemed to be hanging from her seat at an angle. When she opened her eyes, she saw that that was indeed the case. The entire cabin was motionless, though tilted about thirty degrees down toward the airship's bow. There were no engine sounds, though there was a pattering sound. After a moment she realized that she was hearing rain on the *Phoenix's* hull. A glance at the port beside her seat confirmed her guess.

A jab of fear lanced through her. Jame had been in the cockpit. Was he all right? She fumbled with her seat belt. When it unclasped, she almost fell out of her seat. She carefully stepped down and, holding seat backs for support, made her way forward. Before she got to the cockpit, however, it's door swung open. Her heart thumped when she saw Jame lever himself out of the small space. He had a cut over one eye, but he seemed otherwise unharmed.

"Is everyone okay out here?" he asked.

"I think so, yes," Maya said. "Are you?" *An hour ago we were fine. How could this all fall apart so damn quickly?*

"Y-yeah I am, but Cilla banged her head pretty bad. Is Carla all right?" he asked, naming the expedition's doctor, Carla DeCandio.

"I'm fine," Carla said, carefully moving forward along the slanted floor with her bag. "A little shaken up, but okay."

"Great! Can you take a look at her, Doc?" He and the physician disappeared into the cockpit. While they tended to the injured pilot, Maya and Miron took stock of the others. Out of a complement of eight, one was dead: Les Berkowitz, a botanist. Their weapons expert and hunter, Aiko Yokoi, was badly injured, with a broken left leg. She was currently unconscious, having been sedated by Carla. They had been sitting together when the ship crashed, slamming into the bough of a sturdy tree. Les, sitting next to the window, had been speared by a branch through his chest.

Everyone else aside from Cilla sustained only minor injuries, but that was scant comfort.

"We'll have to bury Les," Maya said. "And we need to collect food and supplies... especially medical supplies.

"What about the radio?" Miron asked. "Is it working? We'll need to inform Greensboro. I'm thinking the ship won't fly. Too much damage."

"You're probably right. We're going to have to walk back, looks like."

He grimaced. "That's not going to be any fun. We know next to nothing about the territory between here and there."

It soon developed that the radio was not operating; it was among the instruments that had been smashed in the crash. Peeking into the cockpit, while Carla worked on Cilla Burns, Maya was surprised that Cilla and Jame had survived in the first place.

A grumble of thunder from outside reminded her of the rain. But the storm seemed to be moving off.

We'll have to leave here pretty soon, she thought. Then she realized that it was incumbent on her to help rally the survivors. After all, she was the official liaison with the bionisphere's Information Security team, commonly known as InfoSec, whose agents, known as Monitors, oversaw technology and development in their home bionisphere. Her brother Ahmed was an InfoSec manager who had helped her secure her position during a recent crisis.

Her days as a professor at the university on Eil Malk, as well as her natural knack for organization, had given her plenty of experience in dealing with difficult situations. Right now, she needed all her skills if she meant to get herself and the others back to the Greensboro base alive.

Which meant she needed to focus. Of late, she sometimes had difficulties keeping her mind centered on her tasks. She occasionally struggled with handling day-to-day activities because she couldn't forget what she had learned about the "lives" of the stars.

Maya's life had changed when, over a year ago, she had uncovered the research of Dr. Santos Dumont, a long-dead scientist. Dumont's studies had been suppressed because it represented a stunning challenge to the status quo of the fractured civilization that had dragged itself out of the ruins of the previous centuries. What Dumont had learned had shocked even him: the stars, including Earth's own, were alive. Their thoughts registered as neutrino emissions, and when the emissions increased, it indicated that their vast intellects were growing stronger.

As a result, Maya had come to see human existence as essentially trivial and meaningless. She knew she had to rise above such nihilistic thoughts but often difficulty doing so. These—beings—were so old and so supremely intelligent that it was tempting to visualize them as the true, rightful inhabitants of the galaxy—if not the universe.

All of which made human existence seem rather less important and meaningful to her.

But that was no way to live a life, by allowing yourself to be overwhelmed by feelings of inadequacy. Therefore, Maya did her best to keep such thoughts at bay. Nevertheless, she could never quite ignore the knowledge that these immense and majestic beings, gigantic atomic furnaces that were perhaps the rightful citizens of the universe, crowded the sky in numbers so vast as to be all but meaningless, while caring not a whit for the life on the little balls of rock and gas and ice circling them.

She couldn't help wondering what it must be like to them, basically anchored in one place (even though the stars were not "fixed," in the sense that they did move in relation to one another—but they didn't have physical contact, so there could be no intimacy between them. But such beings probably had no need of that.

Maya sighed. She wasn't getting anything accomplished by indulging in idle speculation. The current situation demanded all her attention. For one thing, they knew relatively little about the land they were going to be crossing for the next few days. They had flown over it, but hadn't seen any settlements, roads, or anything else indicating the presence of human beings.

Yet there had to be settlements somewhere. That they weren't obvious, even from the air, might mean that their inhabitants were keeping themselves under cover. This could be for any number of reasons, but perhaps meant that warlords or hostile tribes were nearby, ready to raid peaceful villages unless those villages were well defended. There could also be solitary brigands, or small bands of robbers. Some had guns, but unless they had a source of ammunition, they were more likely to be armed with spears, bows and arrows, or knives.

More concerning were the occasional pockets of pollution—industrial waste dumps; stockpiles of chemical weapons; old, untended oil storage facilities, now leaking into the ground and rivers; abandoned nuclear reactors—from the Before Times. The inhabitants of the bionispheres knew the locations of all the five hundred or so nuclear plants that had been operating when the asteroid hit. Many had melted down or vanished in terrible steam explosions when their cooling units failed. None of these were deemed safe to approach and would remain dangerous into geologic time.

There were half a dozen fission plants in North Carolina, but none were in their path: Maya had carefully researched their locations before the expedition even departed from Eil Malk. The fifteen or so fusion facilities were not dangerous—but again, they would not be passing near any of these. It was not clear what their condition was now, after so many years of neglect, but no one wanted to get close enough to find out.

Indeed, there would be plenty of other obstacles. Disintegrating structures: collapsed buildings, fallen electrical transmission towers and lines, crumbling highways and bridges clogged with rusting automobiles... from their air they had seen fallow farmlands, some choked with plants that had mutated away from their maintained genetic modifications, and roving bands of formerly domesticated animals now turned wild and predatory. The list of dangers was long and varied. She couldn't keep from thinking about them even as she lashed extra gear to her backpack and helped the others with theirs.

"All right," she said at last, after they had taken stock of their belongings. They stood outside the wrecked aerostat, ignoring the gentle rain, while Cilla and rested inside, out of the drizzle. In addition to Maya, Jame, and Miron, there were Dr. Carla DeCandio, Aiko Yokoi, and Cilla Burns. "Things could be worse. We have weapons, we have food and water, and plenty of purification tablets if we need them, plus portable shelters, first aid materials, and so on. With any luck, we can be home in less than a month, maybe a lot less. What say you?"

"I suggest we camp here for the night," Carla said to Maya. "I'm sure Aiko will be okay, but I'd like her to rest for a day, at least. Plus, I'm a bit worried about Cilla. She isn't responding well to treatment. I'm sure she's sustained a slight concussion. I'd like to give her an x-ray, but we haven't got the equipment."

Maya listened, nodding. "Okay, Doc," she said. "I guess we could all use a rest after what we've been through. Plus, it'll give us more time to go through the *Phoenix* to see if there's anything else we can salvage." She frowned. "But only for tonight, in case anyone living around here comes is attracted by the crash. Okay, everyone, let's get hustle and some tents set up. Is there anything we need right now from inside the ship, before it gets dark?"

Miron raised a hand. "Flares?"

"Good call," Maya said. "I'd forgot about them." She thought for a moment. "We're going to have to carry Aiko for a while until she can walk on that leg. That's going to slow us down." Then something else occurred to her. "By the way, Miron, how is Gabriel?"

"He's okay," Miron said, lifting his memex. Gabriel was an instance of an AI Miron had created not long ago, to bring on the expedition. "I was able to download him from the *Phoenix's* guidance computer just before the crash."

"Good. We're probably going to need him, at least for his maps."

"Yup. He's good to go."

"Well, that's a relief. Okay, we'll get going early tomorrow. The rain should have stopped by then, anyway."

They got busy pitching tents and making a couple of lean-tos where Aiko and Cilla could be more easily watched. Maya occasionally looked over to where the Doctor was tending to Aiko. The Asian woman was something of an enigma to Maya, because although they had never met before being assigned to the ship's crew, there was nevertheless something tantalizingly familiar about her. Maya simply could not put a finger on what it was, and that bothered her. She had a good memory for faces, and she was certain she had never seen Aiko before—but her mind insisted that she must have, sometime, somewhere.

She gave it up. *Oh well—I'll figure it out eventually.*

That night they slept as best they could after having a good meal put together by Carla, who in addition to her medical skills was an enthusiastic amateur cook and made most of the crew's meals out of sheer enjoyment.

THE NEXT MORNING THE rain had indeed stopped falling, which everyone took as an encouraging sign. After finishing up leftovers from the previous night's meal, they broke camp and set out, chatting happily and even singing a little once in a while. According to the map files in Gabriel's memory, their best bet would be to locate old Route 40 and follow that east to Greensboro. The AI claimed that the road was no more than seven kilometers northeast of their current position.

It took them most of the day to find it. Priscilla Burns slowed them down, because she was slightly disoriented after hitting her head and wasn't able to walk very quickly. Also, they were forced to carry Aiko Yokoi on an improvised stretcher, using a blanket strung between two poles. They almost dropped her more than once. Aiko, who had brought along a composite bow and a supply of arrows, insisted on keeping them by her side.

"In case something comes close enough for me to shoot," she said. "We'll be able to use some fresh meat, huh?"

The region was badly overgrown, necessitating the use of machetes to clear a path. Chunks of asphalt were cracked and broken in most places by trees and undergrowth that had been reclaiming the countryside for the past couple of hundred years. In fact, they only stumbled on the road by sheer accident, following coordinates supplied by the AI. GPS systems weren't working, because the satellite net providing the digital information had fallen silent many years before, either because of a breakdown in ground-based network infrastructure, or because the satellites themselves had ceased operating or fallen out of orbit. In any case, the survivors of the crash had to hack their way cross-country, following paths only when these trended in the direction they wished to go.

By the time they came to the road, it was late in the afternoon, and everyone was tired. Rather than continue, they decided to camp by the roadside and go on the next day.

After the meal, Carla took Maya aside while the others were cleaning up. "I'm worried about Cilla," she said quietly. "She's not doing well. I wish we could have stayed where we were for another to give her more time to recuperate."

"Yeah, well, we couldn't really do that, Doc," Maya said. "We were prime targets just sitting there at the crash site. Anyone living nearby would have been drawn to it. I didn't even like saying one night, but we kind of had to. Let's just hope for the best."

Carla nodded, but clearly she wasn't happy. "As you wish," she said.

Everyone who was healthy and mobile—Maya, Jame, Miron, and Carla—agreed to take turns at two-hour watches. Aiko insisted she should be included, but Carla refused to allow it. Jame volunteered for the first, for which Maya was grateful, because she was exhausted. But the second one was hers, and when he woke her she felt as if she'd had no sleep at all. She sat at the fire, listening to the calls of nighttime insects and birds, all of which were so different from what she would have heard on her faraway island home. She felt lonely and anxious. There was a lot of unknown ground to cover between where they were and Greensboro. Angrily she pushed fear and depression away, knowing that she could not show weakness to her comrades. They relied on her to lead them, but she was no better off here than they were. At least they all had weapons.

Hopefully we won't have to use them, she said to herself.

Moodily she poked at the fire with a branch, stirring up the embers. Depression swirled around her like the sparks from the fire. She could not recall being so alone at any other time in her life, and for a moment she was sorely tempted to wake Jame up just so she could have someone to talk to. But she knew she couldn't do that: he was as tired as the rest of them and needed his sleep. Tomorrow would be another long, arduous day.

She glanced toward the lean-to where Aiko and Cilla were sleeping. There was still something naggingly familiar about the Asian woman, and Maya was annoyed with herself because she couldn't figure out how that could be.

Maybe I spotted her at the University once, she thought. *Or saw her in a restaurant or something.* Eventually she had to give it up.

Soon enough it was time to rouse Miron for his turn at watch. She slid into her tent and gratefully stretched out for sleep.

In the morning, they woke to find that Priscilla Burns had died during the night.

Chapter Two -
Touching Down To Earth

The pall of gloom that descended over the remaining survivors as they broke camp after burying Cilla's body remained thick while they shouldered their packs and resumed their trek. Everyone thought she would survive, but, as Doc Carla explained, "She developed a brain bleed overnight. I was afraid that might happen, but I didn't want to say anything, for obvious reasons. Without proper instruments, there was no way I could save her."

"No one blames you," Maya said, putting her arm across Carla's shoulders.

"I know," Carla said, putting her hand atop Maya's. "Doesn't make me feel any better, though. But thanks."

They proceeded in silence for some time. The road was all but impassable in places, between buckled pavement, fallen trees, wrecked vehicles, and rubble from collapsed buildings in what had once been towns or settlements. Even so, it wasn't hard to stay more or less on track even if their progress was slowed by having to carry Aiko in addition to their heavy packs. Throughout the day, Maya and Jame switched off with Carla and Miron. They were frequently forced to stop and rest.

"I'm sorry to be such a damn burden," Aiko said during one such pause.

"It's not your fault; A," Carla said, patting her shoulder. "You'll be okay soon enough. The bone is knitting nicely. Before you know it, you'll be carrying crap like the rest of us."

"The sooner the better," Aiko said. "I feel pretty useless right now."

"Useless?" Maya scoffed. "Without you, we wouldn't be able to keep the guns clean. You know more about them than any of us." Modern weapons, especially the energy weapons, were safe and durable, but even so, they needed to be cleaned every day, especially in a hot and humid environment such as the one in which they were traveling.

She ran a hand along her bow. "I'd love to bring down a deer, maybe."

"I hope you get the chance."

Aiko's other task was to keep track of their progress, which she did by using Miron's AI, Gabriel, balancing the little computer in which it lived on her belly as they slogged along.

"Where are we now?" Miron asked during one of their breaks. They were all tired, sweaty, and grimy.

"Not far from a place called Morganton," Gabriel replied. "We should reach it in three or four days, if we can maintain this pace." Its voice had a rather persnickety tone that Miron claimed sounded amusing, though everyone else found it tiresome. Miron had sampled it from a centuries-old science fiction film soundtrack he found in Eil Malk's digital archives.

"Three or four *days?*" Jame snorted. He swung his machete at a stand of what Gabriel had identified as pokeweed. The stuff wasn't difficult to slice through, but its sap was unpleasant, and, as the AI warned, poisonous.

Maya refused to be daunted. "Come on," she said. "We've all had survival training; we all knew we might have to face something like this."

"Doesn't mean we have to like it," Miron muttered.

"It could be worse," Aiko said from her litter. In addition to her bow, she had a .pistol ready at all times in case something—or someone—attacked the little band. "We could have no food or water. And I could weigh twice what I do."

Even Miron chuckled at that. Aiko was slight and no taller than a twelve-year-old child. She certainly didn't look like the deadliest marksman any of them had ever met.

The weather held, aside from a few late-afternoon thunderstorms that never lasted more than half an hour, and the road maintained a more or less straight course. Gabriel assured them that even though they had to carry Aiko, they were still making ten kilometers per day, sometimes a bit more.

During one of their rests, Aiko motioned Maya over to her litter. Maya squatted down.

"What's on your mind, Ay?"

"I don't know if you've noticed or not," the Asian woman said quietly, "but the road has been basically cleared of debris for the last five kilometers or so."

Maya shrugged. "I hadn't really, but come to think of it, yeah; you're right. So?"

"So I wonder why. And who might have done it. We haven't seen any sign of anyone living around here, but it looks to me that someone has been keeping the road passable for some reason. All I'm saying is, stay alert."

"You think we're in danger?"

It was Aiko's turn to shrug. "I can't say for sure, but let's not take anything for granted. I would have expected to see some signs at least of large animals. Bears, wildcats maybe. But there's nothing. Of course, I'm confined to this stretcher and can't do my usual scouting trip into the woods, but still—I find it rather odd. It makes me feel..." She wriggled her fingers. "Antsy." She taped the pistol, which was sitting on the stretcher by her side.

"Okay, you're the expert. I'll pass the word."

"Thanks, Maya."

But whatever the source was of Aiko's heightened awareness, noting troubling manifested itself over the next couple of days. By that time, they had walked about eighty kilometers from the crash site, which everyone agreed was quite a feat. True, they were nearly exhausted, but the realization that they were making better time than they had expected gave them heart.

Around mid-afternoon of the sixth day following the crash, they passed through the silent ruins of what had been the town of Morganton. It was clear that no-one lived there now. Houses and stores had collapsed without being repaired, and the forest had reclaimed most of what might once have been a thriving town. On the whole, they found the site, and the sight, discouraging.

There was no point in scrounging through the ruins for anything that might have been missed by human and animals. Too much time had passed.

As they were leaving the deserted town behind, Aiko spoke up. "Hold it," she said between her teeth. "Something's—"

A strange whizzing sound interrupted her. Carla swore and clapped her hand to her left arm. Blood trickled between her clenched fingers. "I'm hit," she said in an almost conversational tone. A short, stubby dart protruded from her flesh.

Maya swore as well. "Take cover!" she shouted. As they hurried into the undergrowth off the road, she was sharply aware that their unknown adversaries had at least a couple of number of advantages over them: they doubtless knew the territory, and they probably outnumbered the islanders.

No matter: Maya knew they had to try to escape, no matter what. Savage yips and cries followed them as they penetrated further into the dense foliage.

"Doc?" Maya flung over her shoulder.

"Flesh wound," came the terse reply. "Didn't hit an artery. I'm okay."

Looking at the bolt, which was still stuck in the doctor's arm, Maya said, "You want me to pull that out for you?"

"No. Obviously it isn't poisoned, or I'd be dead already. And removing it will just make it bleed worse. Leave it for now. I have a pretty high pain tolerance, Maya. Let's keep moving!"

Maya didn't bother to respond. Perspiration poured down her face while she slashed her way through the vegetation with her machete, doing her best to clear the stuff away as quickly as possible before their unknown assailants caught up with them.

Now they heard more shouts behind them. Something odd...

"Maya? Those are all women," Aiko said through gritted teeth. Being bounced and jostled round had to be extremely painful for her, but she was doing her job as best she could, analyzing the situation and trying to determine the nature of their enemies.

"What? Women?" Maya couldn't spare breath for more.

"Yes... maybe half a dozen. I don't hear any male voices. Look, we can stop and fight. I'm ready, got my guns and bow here. If all *they* have is crossbows, we might have an edge over them."

A crumbling stone wall loomed out of the greenery, blocking their path. It was too tall to climb, especially burdened as they were with Aiko. "What the—?" She took it in at a glance. "Miron—go left. Jame, right. Find us a way in or around this damn wall! Aiko and the doc and I will hold 'em off as long as we can."

"But—"

"Jame, *don't argue*. Please. Hon. Do what I say!"

"...Yup. On it." The men dove into the bushes along the wall.

"Aiko? Give Carla one of your pistols."

Though the doctor generally did not carry a weapon, Maya had no concerns about the Doc's ability to wield a gun, even injured as she was; mission requirements meant that all of them had to qualify as marksmen.

The shouts were growing closer.

"What do these bitches want with us?" Aiko wondered aloud in a strained voice.

"The usual things robbers want, I suppose," Maya said absently. She wiped sweat from her forehead.

She jumped as someone touched her arm. It was Jame. "Gate, this way," he said, tugging to her left.

"Okay, great. Doc? We're leaving." She and Carla took up the stretcher and followed Jame, forcing their way through briars and clinging vines, ignoring lacerations. The effort made Carla's wound bleed more freely, but for now there was little they could do about it.

"Where's Miron?" Carla gritted between clenched teeth.

"I dunno," Jame said from up ahead. "We'll find him, don't worry."

Moments later they came to a rusted gate, with gaps in its bars. It wouldn't keep their attackers out, but it might delay them easier to pick off if they followed the islanders. Maya ignored her fear that the outlaw women probably knew about this place.

I hope it isn't their hideout! She almost laughed. *That would be funny...*

Inside the gate, they found themselves on the overgrown grounds of what might once have been an estate. Visible through the vegetation that had taken over the landscape were some low buildings. Maya revised her first impression: maybe this was a school or some other sort of facility.

But there was no time to wonder about that. Their pursuers were getting nearer. Soon they'd find the gate. Maya helped bind Carla's wound a little better, but the doctor still refused to allow her to pull the bolt out. She and Maya positioned themselves behind trees, keeping their weapons aimed at the entry. Aiko propped herself up against another tree, gun ready.

Maya whirled around at the sound of footsteps behind them. Then she lowered her gun. "Damn, Miron."

"Huh? Listen, I found a gate around the other side. It was closed, but unlocked, so I—"

"Later, all right? Listen, go back and make sure no one gets in that way."

"But I found something else."

"I said *later*."

"Okay, okay." He dashed off.

"Doc, see if you and Jame can get us into one of those buildings? These crazy ladies are gonna be here any minute. Aiko and I will hold then off."

"Right." Carla and Jame disappeared into the bushes, heading toward the ruins.

"How much trouble are we in, do you think?" Maya asked Aiko after the others were gone.

"Maybe a lot, if we can't get to a better defensive position. We have a good bit of ammo, but out here we're exposed."

"Yeah."

Maya didn't take her eyes off the area near the gate. Sure enough, the underbrush there suddenly shook, just a little. Narrowing her eyes, Maya snapped off a shot, and was rewarded with a cry of pain. *That gave them something to think about.*

Jame came into view through the brush. "We found a way in," he said.

"Thank god!" Carrying Aiko, they stumbled along the rough trail Jame had made minutes earlier.

"I don't know what this place used to be," he said, "but it's definitely kind of weird."

"I don't care, as long as we can defend it from those people out there."

"Shouldn't be that hard. We can barricade the entrance and hide behind the walls. They can't get to us without showing themselves."

She soon discovered he was right. Inside the single-story building he had entered were scraps of furniture and what looked to have been electronic devices of some kind. There were gaps in the ceiling and walls, the windows lacked glass, and everything was water damaged. Plants had taken root in what was left of the carpet. Creepers and vines climbed the walls. The place smelled of animals and disuse.

"Homey," Aiko said, wrinkling her nose. "Come on; prop me up over there against the wall where I have a clear shot at the door."

Maya positioned the crippled weapons expert as requested, making sure her weapons were close at hand, then she and the others took up positions using as much cover as possible. It wasn't much. Meanwhile, Carla opened their first aid kit and gave some attention to her injury. She had grown very pale, but after allowing Maya to remove the crossbow bolt, Carla cleansed and bandaged the wound and swallowed a couple of pain pills.

"That's more like it she said." Her color was already returning.

"If they get in here, they'll pick us off easily," Maya said.

"Yes!" Miron pumped his fist in the air.

"What?" Maya turned to look at her former student, who was tapping away at his computer. "Miron, what the hell are you doing?"

"Let me show you something," he said, and as he spoke, there was a loud thud from somewhere else in the building.

Maya froze. "They've breached the wall!"

"No, no," Miron said. "That wasn't the people chasing us. Here!" He scrambled through the rubble littering the floor and thrust his laptop at her.

"I don't have time for—"

"Dammit, Maya, will you just *look*?"

On the screen, she saw wavering view of what looked to be a room very similar to the one in which they were cowering. The view trembled, and simultaneously they felt another heavy thud.

Aiko looked around fearfully. "Is the ceiling caving in?"

Lines of information and code scrolled across the bottom of the screen. "This is interfaced with its onboard cameras," Miron said speaking so quickly she could barely understand him. "I found the thing a few rooms down, powered down? And thought Gabriel might be able to acquire it in his network."

"Miron. *What the hell are you talking about?*"

Another thud—closer.

"Mayaaaa?" from the Doc, clearly alarmed.

"There's something out there," Jame said tightly, raising his gun.

"Don't shoot it," Miron said as debris crunched outside in the hallway. "Gabriel has it completely under control. I don't know how it could still have power after all this time, but it's got banks of solar cells, and when the roof fell in, it probably started soaking up sunlight for its batteries. I don't know, but I do know it's operational."

"*What* is operational?" Maya demanded just as something pushed in the door.

"That," Miron said, pointing.

Aiko bit off a shriek; Carla gasped, Jame swore. Maya, struck speechless, could only stare open-mouthed as *something* pushed into the room.

It was tall, so tall that it had to crouch to get through the door. Two-legged, it had two arms that were about the size of a man's, and a large claw on the second toe of each foot. It was either armored or made of metal, but metal streaked with bird droppings and discolored by stains. It showed no obvious sign of rust, but its left leg seemed to be damaged, because it staggered or limped as it entered the room. Aiko fired at it—the bullet spanged off.

"Don't shoot! Don't shoot!" Miron shouted. "It's totally harmless!" And sure enough, the thing made no move toward them, merely stood, with green lights flickering in unison in its eye sockets.

"Sure doesn't look that way," Maya barked. "What the hell *is* that thing, Miron?"

"Well, I'm not exactly sure, but I can tell you that Gabriel is controlling it. When I was making my way through the hallways, you know, climbing over wreckage and so on, I saw a glitter of light in one of the rooms. This guy was in there. I mean, I figured right away that it was a robot of some kind. There was a little red indicator light blinking on the right side of its neck...see?"

Maya peered at the thing, which really did look like a chrome-plated or stainless-steel dinosaur of some kind. She rifled through her memory, which had been augmented during her time with the Monitors back on Eil Malk. But there was nothing in her mental library about anything like this bizarre machine.

Mirin said, "So I thought, if it still has power, and if it *is* computer activated, well, maybe Gabriel could pick it up. He can do that... he can take control of, like, peripheral units, right? Same as a computer logging in to a wireless network and taking over another computer. Which happened all the time in the old days, we know. Malware attacks on infrastructure, and all that sort of thing. You've heard of that, right?"

Maya nodded. She was familiar with such terminology because her younger brother, Ahmed, worked for Eil Malk's Information and Security team, commonly known as InfoSec. In fact, she worked for them now, as well, having followed Ahmed into the service. As a member of InfoSec, she no longer had to chafe under the strictures the agency placed on most academics, preventing them from researching scientific methodologies and discoveries that lead up to the disaster of 2173 that came perilously close to obliterating all life on the planet. InfoSec was finally loosening its grip a little, which was why it promoted and funded this expedition to the lost continent.

"But Miron—what is the *point?*" Jame demanded.

"Maybe it can help us," Miron said. "Who knows what's in its memory banks? Besides, we need to do something about those women out there, right?"

As if to underscore his remark, there was a shout from somewhere outside the building. Their enemies were closing in.

"Can you scare them away with this?" Maya asked, gesturing at the robot.

"Worth a try, right?" Miron tapped at his little computer's keyboard and spoke a few code words. "Okay—I've uploaded a copy of Gabriel into this thing's memory. There's barely enough room, but I downloaded some of its operating system into my computer, so enough of Gabriel should fit in to give him total control. Because he needs to be autonomous... before, I was running the thing like I was playing a video game." He typed rapidly. "Okay, he's in. *Now* we ought to see something."

The robot tossed its head, opened its mouth—which was filled with small, serrated metal teeth—and emitted a roar. Everyone jumped, but Miron said, "Relax, it's just Gabriel trying out the sound system."

"Affirmative," the dinosaur said. Or rather, Gabriel said, using a speaker embedded in the thing's throat. The robot could not move its mouth to speak and had no tongue in any case.

It turned and lumbered out of the room.

"Are you sure that monstrosity is working properly?" Jame asked, "It seems to be damaged."

"Yeah, well, it's been sitting here for who knows *how* long, day in and day out, season after season, for years and years. I'm kind of surprised it moves at all. Someone did a great job with its design."

Outside the room, they heard the dinosaur's uneven steps as it moved toward the invaders. It roared and shrieked. "Ought to give them a good scare if nothing else," Miron said. "Gather round." He set the computer on a table in front of Aiko, and his companions crowded in to watch.

The view was obviously from the robot. "Cameras in its head," Miron confirmed. The view jumped and jiggled as the mechanism made its way out of the building and into the foliage. Branches and leaves whipped past.

"Can their crossbow bolts harm it?" Maya asked Miron.

"I don't think so, and they don't have any energy weapons like my handgun, but we'll make this quick, just in case."

"What kind of dinosaur is it supposed to be, anyway?" asked Aiko.

Gabriel answered in its usual flat voice. "It is a model of *utahraptor ostrommaysorum,*" said the computer.

"Well, that tells me exactly nothing," Jame said with a grin.

"This would be a young, immature male," Gabriel went on. "Adults gained a length of 16 feet, approximately. This model was designed to be part of a roaming family unit for an audio animatronic exhibit of some type. The adult models have not survived, though their ID signatures are in the young one's memory matrix."

"Which means," Miron said, "that if we ever find them, Gabriel can probably acquire them, too."

Maya blinked. "Whoa, time out. Are we in part of an amusement park or something?"

"I believe so," said Gabriel. "This would appear to have been a research facility for the park, many years ago. All the other attractions have crumbled to ruins."

"Hey," Jame said, gesturing at the screen. "Something's happening."

The robot had left the grounds of the facility by pushing open the gate through which they had gained entry and was moving toward a group of five adult females. They were clad in skins and makeshift protective gear, with feathers stuck in their hair and tattoos or war paint on their faces. All of them carried crossbows, with quivers for the bolts on their backs. They also had knives in sheaths on their hips.

"Did you tell it to go out?" Maya asked Miron.

"I am guiding it," Gabriel answered before Miron could speak. "You do want to be rid of these people, do you not?"

"Yes," said Maya.

"Very well. I have gained more understanding of this mechanism's features."

Maya had an idea. "See if you can capture one of them, Gabriel, without harming her too much."

"Affirmative."

The view started moving more quickly as the robot, under Gabriel's guidance, began stalking the women who had been talking Maya's comrades.

"They see it," Aiko said.

The women took on defensive postures. Two of them made as if to flee, but one of the women—who had more facial tattoos than the others—yelled at them. "Hold ground! Art fearful?" She said this with deepest scorn. "Ye are nay of my crew, then. Hold, I say!"

"But, but... look you! Look at it!" said one of the women who wanted to run. "What is it?"

"A machine of the old times," said the headwoman. "A brainless device, no more."

Miron grinned. "Brainless, eh?" He pressed a key on his computer. Pitching his voice low, he bellowed, "A device, am I? Lay down your arms and depart this place at once!" His words blatted out from the robot dinosaur's eternal speaker at high volume.

The headwoman wheeled around and gazed up at the approaching monster, her face reflecting a mixture of fury, fear, and wonder. "I hight Aly Lynxclaw," she yelled, "and I give ground for no walking toolbox!"

"We'll soon see about that, intruder!"

Two of the women, the ones who had wanted to run, quivered in their places, but apparently they were more afraid of Aly Lynxclaw than they were of the robot. It advanced, clawed hands upraised, treading heavily so that the earth shook a little. Lynxclaw swore and loosed a crossbow bolt at the oncoming beast, but it clanged off its metal hide.

She stood her ground, but behind her the two fearful ones broke and fled through the trees. Lynxclaw stayed where she was and yanked a spear out of the scabbard at her back.

In full control, Miron, with tongue sticking out from his lips in concentration, reached out and grabbed the spear. To her credit, the headwoman refused to relinquish it: instead, she tried to tug it out of the thing's grasp, but the robot was too strong. Instead, it snatched her other arm, gripping it firmly so that no matter how much she struggled, Aly Lynxclaw could not free herself.

"Miron!" Maya said. "Bring her back here. Let's see if we can talk some sense into her."

"Very well, I—" But the rest of his sentence was interrupted when a large rock struck the robot's head with a staggering impact. It dropped Aly Lynxclaw. Miron, frantically working the controls, saw that "he" had been ambushed by one of Lynxclaw's gang.

"Damn, she got away," Jame said. Disarmed now, Lynxclaw backed away from the animatronic dinosaur.

Moving quickly, Miron had the robot make a grab for the newcomer—and, to everyone's surprise, he got her. But he had misjudged the thing's strength, for she shrieked in pain.

"Uh-oh—I think I broke her arm," Miron said. He was sweating profusely.

It was too much even for the intrepid Aly Lynxclaw, for she fled after the others, leaving the behind the woman who had attacked the robot, twisting about in its iron grip.

Chapter Three -
Fighting For Survival

"**S**top struggling," Miron said via the speaker. "You can't get loose, and you'll only injure yourself more." To everyone's surprise, the woman ceased her efforts to free herself.

"Let me go, fiend," she growled. They saw on screen that she was perhaps not even five feet tall. Her spiky black hair was done in what had once been called a crew cut and was very short on the sides. She wore a leather skirt divided into panels and decorated with metal studs, a similar leather waistcoat with metal breastplates, and a metal skullcap. A short sword was buckled at her waist, and a coil of rope. Her wrists and forearms were protected by intricately wrought bracelets, as were her upper arms around her biceps, which were marked with crude tattoos. On her feet were tall, laced Romanesque sandals. There were scars on her face, but they were regular and appeared to have been done deliberately. Despite her short stature, she was well-muscled and looked every inch a warrior.

"I don't think so," Miron said. "We want to talk to you."

In response she spat so accurately at the robot that her spittle obscured one of its eyes.

"Nice shot," Jame murmured. "That's some expectorating."

"Bring her in," Carla said to Miron. "But don't hurt her. I want to have a look at her arm."

The robot had to all but drag its captive, panting from her exertions to free herself, back to the gate, where Jame, Carla, and Miron were waiting. Jame stood guard at the gate with the robot in case there was another attack from the female brigands while Carla and Miron brought the prisoner into the facility.

"I wish we'd had time to look around," Carla groused as they tied the captive to a chair. "There must be a medical office here somewhere."

Maya scoffed. "Do you really think there'd be anything useful in it even if there is?"

"No, not really, but I'd like to check, anyway." To the prisoner, she said, "I'm a doctor. May I look at your arm? I'm sure it's very painful."

The limb was red and swollen, and obviously hurt. "Go ahead," the woman snarled.

"Let's see what we can do, shall we?"

Her sure, gentle touch seemed to calm the woman, who relaxed a little.

"I'm Carla," said the doctor, as she carefully probed the limb. "What's your name?"

"I hight Blue Petal," said the woman, and hissed in pain as Carla checked her injury.

"Forgive me," Carla said. "I don't mean to hurt you. Well, Blue Petal—what an interesting name, by the way—the good news is, it's not broken. You have what we call a metaphyseal fracture of the upper part of your left ulna. I can strap it up for you and give you some pain medication."

She looked puzzled. "What is... an ulna?"

"Well, it's one of the long bones in your forearm," Carla said, and held out her own arm. "It sort of twists around, which allows you to have a range of radial motion." She flipped her wrist back and forth to demonstrate.

The islanders kept their weapons trained on her while Carla bandaged and splinted Blue Petal's arm. When she was finished, the captive turned it this way and that.

"I must admit, you did a good job. Our own doctor couldn't have done better."

Carla frowned. "Thanks, but *I* could have, if I had any proper equipment here," she said while packing up her supplies.

Blue Petal eyed them all in turn. "You speak oddly," she said. "I have not heard the like of your accents." She added, staring at Aiko, "I *have* seen pictures of people who look like you, lady, with your eyes, but only in some of the old books we have."

Aiko shrugged at her comrades. "We're all from an island far from here," she said. "My ancestors came from a place even farther away, called Japan. From what we saw, your people are all Caucasians."

"Caucasians?"

"White people, like Maya and Jame."

"Oh, yes. Well, we do have some black folk in our tribes, like your doctor, here; but none were with us when we encountered you."

"Listen, Blue Petal, we are not your enemies," Maya said, crouching down in front of her chair. "We were... marooned in an accident and are trying to get back to our friends in Greensboro. Do you know where that is?"

"I have heard of it," was the reply. "It is some days to the east."

"That's right. Can you tell us about conditions between here and there?"

"Conditions?"

"Yes," Jame said. "You know, Are there robbers? Threats from animals?"

Blue Petal shrugged. To Maya, she said, "There are always those things. There have always been those things, for as long as any of us can remember." She looked at Jame, then back to Maya. "We do not let our men speak for us."

Maya exchanged glances with the others. "Well, we do. We are all equals in our land."

Blue Petal frowned. "Men are strong, and good for some things, but when it comes to making decisions for the tribe, we listen to what they have to say, but the woman make all the choices."

Miron suppressed a chuckle, but he subsided when Maya glared at him.

"Sorry," he muttered.

Blue Petal, noting this, nodded. "The young ones, especially," she said.

Miron turned red while his comrades laughed.

"And you are how old?" Maya asked.

"Sixteen."

"Ohhh. Well, that explains a lot."

Blue Petal frowned. "What is that supposed to mean?"

"Never mind, sorry."

The tribeswoman gave her a sharp look, but all she said was, "Tell me about the metal dragon. These buildings are accursed, so we never go in them. I am accounted brave among my peers, but that thing..." She shuddered. "How have you made it move? Is it from the Old Days?"

Jame frowned. "The... Old Days? Maya, do you suppose she means the Dark Years?" That was how the islanders referred to the span of time following the asteroid impact, while civilization crawled back from the brink of total ruin.

Maya shrugged. "Same difference," she said. To Blue Petal, she said, "Listen. If you can guide us safely out of this region and make sure we're on the right road to Greensboro, we'll let you go after a while." She looked at her fellows. "Let's talk about this. Excuse us, Blue Petal." She led the others out of the room to another one down the hall. This one was as cluttered with debris as the first one.

Miron wrinkled his nose. "What a mess! Oh well, we'll only be here for a day or so, right?"

"As far as I know," Maya said. "But anyway—what about Blue Petal? What do you all think, can we trust her?"

"I don't know about that," Carla said. "She's a lot calmer now, and I'm sure she's grateful to us for fixing her arm, at least so some extent.

But who knows? We don't know anything about her people or her or their way of life. They could be watching us right now, for all we know. They obviously have better woodcraft than we do."

"It seems pretty obvious to me that they are scavengers and thieves," Jame said. "They tried to rob us, and they shot Carla."

"So you don't think we should let her go, then," Maya said. It wasn't a question.

"No, I do not."

Doctor Carla lifted her good arm. "Suppose we brought her along with us?"

Miron nodded thoughtfully. "You mean, as a hostage, like? So that those other nutty females don't attack us? I'd go for that. I think Gabriel could keep an eye on her. If we keep her hands tied, or let the dragon guard her. I mean, he never sleeps. He'll alert us if she tries anything."

Carla, Jame and Aiko nodded. "We don't need the responsibility of caring for her," Aiko said. "It works for me. Someone's going to have to keep an eye on her, though, so she doesn't try to escape."

Miron crossed his arms over his chest. "We can have the dragon do that. Like I said. Gabriel can watch her even if we're all asleep."

"Okay," Maya said. "I don't like the idea of keeping someone tied up, but the dragon can do it. Say, we ought to give it a name. We can't keep calling it 'the dragon.'"

"It isn't really supposed to even *be* a dragon," Aiko said. "Is it? It's a dinosaur. But how about this? In Japanese mythology, Guanyin is a Bodhisattva—"

Jame said, "Wait, what? What's a, a, what'd you call it?"

"A Bodhisattva," Aiko said patiently. "A person who is on the path toward enlightenment."

"Oh, all right. I guess."

"Anyway, the Bodhisattva Guanyin is sometimes shown riding a white dragon, or even turning into one. He's associated with compassion. So let's call our dinosaur Guanyin, or even Yin, maybe."

Maya nodded. "Sure, that'll do, I guess. Short, easy to remember. Everyone? Any problem with calling our buddy Yin?"

There were no objections. They all set about clearing some space for themselves in the ruins. Although everyone agreed that it made sense for Yin to stand guard over Blue Petal, Maya vetoed that suggestion. "I want him to patrol the grounds," she said. "He can move pretty quietly, he can see in the dark, and he'll scare the devil out of anyone who comes snooping around. He sure seems to scare Blue Petal. As to her, we'll have to take turns guarding her, at least until we leave. I think we can trust her, but she could just as easily be stringing us along in the hope that her tribeswoman will rescue her. I have no ill will against them—"

"Yeah, well, *I* sure do," Carla said, rubbing her bandaged arm.

"Understandable. Anyway, as I was saying... I have *hardly* any ill will against them, but that doesn't mean we should just assume all is well. We'll get some rest now and set out tomorrow. How does that sound to everyone?"

"Sure."

"Agreed."

"Yeah, why not?"

Aiko said, "I'll go with the consensus."

"Good," said Maya. "All right; let's get some food together, shall we? I am suddenly realizing that I am bloody well *starving*."

LATER THAT EVENING, after having a good meal—even Blue Petal, who wasn't used to the island-type food they had brought along, which tended to be dried fish, vegetables, and rice, augmented with some canned meat from their supplies, said it was more than palatable—everyone felt much better. Carla's arm wasn't galling her as much, though she declared that was because of the pain killers. Blue Petal's hands were untied, but not her legs, until after they allowed her to relieve herself, for which she was grateful.

No one wanted to stay up late, so they turned in shortly after eating. Throughout the night, Maya, always a light sleeper, was awakened by the sound of something moving through the underbrush, but by the occasional glimpse she had of something glowing red and yellow, she knew she was seeing the running lights along Yin's flanks, to which Gabriel had alerted them earlier. He had discovered them while running diagnostics on Yin's operating system. Comforted by the thought of the indefatigable robot making its rounds, Maya easily fell back into slumber.

All in all, despite the interruptions she slept well. When she awoke, slightly before the others, she started their small portable stove going and made coffee and tea. Outside it was raining gently.

Not the nicest day, she said to herself, enjoying the quiet and solitude of being the only one awake. *But we have to get the hell out of here before Aly Lynx-lady or whatever her name is decides to try to pull off a rescue attempt for Blue Petal.*

After breaking their fast, the party set out, with Yin taking point. By common consent, they gave him most of their packs to carry, being careful to strap them onto him so that he wasn't off-balance. Even though they were relieved of carrying their gear, the group's progress was necessarily slow, because Yin and the humans had to pick their way over rubble, fallen trees, and tangles of vegetation that entirely obscured the road in places. Blue Petal's hands were bound behind her back, but she didn't seem to be overly resentful. She was clearly wary of Yin and did her best to keep as far from the robot as she could.

"The resilience of youth," Carla muttered to Maya as they walked along the old roadway.

Jame was walking beside the captive to keep an eye on her. He asked, "Why haven't your people kept this clear, Blue Petal?"

"We have our pathways through the forest. There are also game trails that we use. This old road... well, it would take a lot of effort to remove all the junk. There aren't enough of us to need such a road. Plus, leaving all the obstacles means no one can sneak up on us from this way."

"That makes sense, I guess," Maya said.

Though they all had their weapons at the ready, nothing seemed eager to attack them. The heat and humidity grew as the day wore on, until they all, even Blue Petal, were dripping with perspiration. Luckily, most of the road was shaded by the trees. Once they passed over a small river, using a concrete and metal bridge that was crumbling but seemed sturdy enough. Blue Petal assured them that the bridge was secure, but even so, they didn't dawdle, crossing it as quickly as they could.

At one point Maya dropped back with Jame, and said quietly, "I find it a little odd that our little wild girl is coming with us so willingly."

"I hadn't thought about it," he replied. "But maybe. Yeah, maybe she's a bit docile. Do you think she's expecting a rescue attempt?"

"I don't know *what* to think. But we better stay alert, especially with Aiko still unable to walk. Carla says she's doing well, but even so, she'll need crutches once she gets off that stretcher, at least for a week or so. It's really going to slow us down."

"Agreed. I don't know what we can do about that, though."

They kept to as steady a pace as they could throughout the day, and by the time the sun was setting and they halted for the night they had covered another ten kilometers or so from the abandoned amusement park. Their supper was particularly good because Blue Petal pointed out a number of edible plants she spotted growing wild along the road, and Carla incorporated these into a delicious stew.

The night passed without incident.

The next day, they woke to find that the weather had cleared, and there was less humidity. They resumed their march in good spirits. Swinging along at an energetic pace, Maya had time to wonder at their surroundings. How long had it been since anyone had lived around here? Blue Petal, when questioned, either didn't know or wasn't saying. What would the former inhabitants think if they saw the little band trooping through these little towns: three Caucasian islanders; an Asian woman on a stretcher; a short-haired scowling barbarian woman with tattoos and facial scars, carrying a spear; black female physician; and an eight-foot-tall chrome-plated robotic dinosaur.

Your basic tourists, Maya said to herself, grinning.

The roadway remained more or less clear. Trees had taken root through the pavement in places, cracking the asphalt, but apart from that and occasional wreckage and patches of overgrown vegetation, it had held up remarkably well given the amount of time that had passed.

Shortly after mid-morning, Yin began emitting a grating sound while walking. They paused while Miron had Gabriel go through the animatronic beast's circuits and systems.

"You just did that yesterday, I thought," Maya said while he peered at the screen of his little hand-held memex.

He shot her an exasperated look. "Well, I did, yes, but that was before we took Yin out of his normal environment and put him to work guarding the perimeter of our camp, and then using him as a pack animal. That last, especially, isn't what he was designed for. The extra weight is probably too much for his joints. Plus, as an amusement park attraction, or whatever he was, he never had to clamber over debris or pick his way through dense vegetation. We're asking a lot of him."

Maya nodded slowly. "Understood. Can he be fixed?"

"I'm sure he can, but that probably requires tools and equipment that we left behind. Spare parts, too, most likely. I mean, *I'm* not set up to take him apart and find out what's wrong; not in the middle of the road, anyway." He shrugged.

After some grumbling, most of Yin's packs were removed and handed back to their original carriers, who shouldered them with relatively good grace. Only Aiko's gear was left on the robot. This reduction of weight seemed to benefit Yin, whose joints no longer creaked as he walked.

"Just as I thought," Miron said. "We were asking too much of him."

"Do you think we did any permanent damage to him?"

Miron shrugged.

Although no one was happy about having to lug their belongings again, they did appreciate having had something of a reprieve. But soon enough they were all drenched in perspiration. The sole good thing to come out of that episode was that Blue Petal suggested they rig a travois for Aiko.

"That way," she said, "you wouldn't have to tire yourselves out carrying her stretcher."

The islanders looked at one another. "What's a travois?" Maya asked.

"It's something the American Indians used to use to carry loads," the barbarian said. She went on to explain that its basic construction consisted of a platform or netting mounted on two long poles, lashed in the shape of an A-frame.

"You drag it, with the pointed end forward," she said. "In fact, you could probably harness it to Yin and let him do it. If he's strong enough. With his bad joints, and all."

Miron was nodding as she spoke. "It's certainly worth a try."

"Hey," said Carla, "what if we found a couple of wheels and mounted them at the end? That way it wouldn't have to be dragged. And it would probably be a smoother ride for Aiko."

Everyone liked the idea. No wheels were immediately at hand, and a quick search turned up none in the general rubble along the road, but the travois itself was easily made, from poles cut from nearby saplings. And, when it was harnessed to Yin, the dinobot had no trouble dragging the extra weight.

"I guess it's easier for him, since it's closer to his center of gravity," Miron said in approval, as they gave the contrivance a short trial. Aiko pronounced it fairly comfortable, even though she ended up lying at an angle to the ground and had to be strapped in, to keep from falling out.

"Wheels would sure help, though," she said. "It's kind of a bumpy ride."

"We'll keep an eye out for some," Jame said.

None turned up, though. Even so, the travois made things easier for everyone except possibly Aiko, and she wasn't one to complain.

Chapter Four - Barbaric Decisions

Shortly before they meant to make camp for the night, Blue Petal, who was walking toward the rear of the group with Jame, suddenly said, "Stop. Everyone, stop where you are."

"What's the matter?" Jame asked.

Blue Petal shushed him. The islanders stood still, listening, shaking their heads at each other in puzzlement.

"Take cover!" Blue Petal said. She dashed to the side of the road. The others followed suit. Miron had Gabriel direct Yin off the road, under a curtain of kudzu.

They crouched, sweating, with muscles taut, waiting for whatever was coming. Maya shared a glance with Jame, who was next to her. "Should we free her hands?" she whispered.

Jame chewed his lips for a few moments. Then he blew out his breath. "Yeah, I say we risk it. If she runs, well, she runs. Otherwise she's another person who can fight."

Maya nodded. She crawled over to Blue Petal, took out her clasp knife, and cut the barbarian's bonds.

Blue Petal nodded at her. "Where's my crossbow?" she muttered.

Maya pointed at Aiko. "In her pack. Hey, A!" she hissed in a stage whisper. "Give Blue's bow back to her."

Aiko looked doubtful for a moment, then scrabbled in her pack, which was lashed to the travois beside her. She took out Blue Petal's crossbow and handed it over, along with its quiver of bolts.

"Thank you," Blue Petal murmured to Maya. "Trust me."

"Yeah, well—we have to. Now tell me what's going on."

"They are," Blue Petal said, pointing with her chin out at the roadway.

To their left, back the way they had come, Maya saw a group of half a dozen bearded men come trotting down the road. They were armed with spears, crossbows, knives, and swords.

"Bear Clan," Blue Petal said quietly. "See the bear claw necklaces?"

Maya squinted. Sure enough, each of the men, all of whom were dressed similarly to Blue Petal in skins and leather, wore a necklace of large bear claws around his neck.

"They seek to enslave us," she went on. "They never have enough women. That's because they're cruel and lazy. They make the women do all the work, then they rape them into the bargain. I'd rather die than let them catch me. My sisters and I don't go looking for trouble, but if we run across one of their hunting parties, we do our best to kill them all. Or at least castrate them. Because of what they would do if they caught us."

Maya's eyes went wide, but she said nothing.

Blue Petal crawled from one person to another, speaking barely above a whisper. "Dangerous men. Smart and vicious. They want women."

Jame drew in a sharp breath. "Do we fight them?"

"Only if we can win."

Aiko drew a chunky-looking gun out of her pack. It had coils around its muzzle, which ended in a lens rather than a hole. "I can fire once every ten seconds with this," she said.

Blue Petal shrugged. "I know not what it is."

"Laser pistol. Zap!"

The barbarian shrugged again.

Aiko grinned at her. "You'll see."

The approaching men were moving almost soundlessly, which led Maya to wonder how Blue Petal had known they were there?

But there was no time to wonder about that now, because the clan men had almost reached the place where the islanders were hidden.

Suddenly one of them shouted. "Look there!"

Oh, bloody hell, Maya thought in dismay. *They've spotted Yin.*

Sure enough, the men immediately formed a semi-circle around the dinosaur, which stood motionless in its cloak of kudzu on the other side of the road. For an instant, Maya harbored the hope that they would be frightened off, but before anything like that could happen, Blue Petal had taken matters into her own hands by firing at the men. Her bolt struck one in the back of his head, and he dropped.

The men whirled and began firing bolts of their own into the underbrush where the islanders were concealed.

"Dammit, Blue!" Maya spat, but she was too busy defending herself to say anything else. A smoking crater appeared in one man's breast: the result of a laser beam from Aiko's gun. The weapon wasn't as effective as its ancient space-based brethren had once been, but at short range and even in air it could kill at short range. The man shrieked and fell to his knees, moaning.

Miron, with great presence of mind, now brought Yin into the fray. The bot stalked out from cover, roaring fearsomely, lights blinking. Cursing and yelling, the marauders were forced to divide their attention, caught as they now were in the open between two foes. And they had already lost one man, who lay motionless on the road.

Two of them faced the oncoming dino, while the other three kept firing into the underbrush. "These people aren't very bright," Jame ground out, as he took aim with his pistol and fired. The bullet caught one clansman in the leg. He screeched and stumbled in his tracks. The biggest man, who was apparently the leader, threw his spear at Yin, then bawled out an order to retreat. They grabbed the injured one and bolted back the way they had come, leaving the dead man. The islanders fired after them to supply incentive. Jame apparently hit one, who staggered, but kept running.

Blue Petal nodded approvingly. She emerged from the bushes and stalked over to the dead man. Looking down at him, she spat in his face, then kicked him savagely in the ribs.

"Pig," she said. "Son of pigs." She did a little dance where she stood.

Somewhat bemused, Maya watched Blue Petal's triumphant jig. It occurred to her that they were going to have to do something about Blue Petal. It didn't seem practicable to keep the young barbarian woman a captive any longer, especially since she had proven herself to be valuable: her ability to survive in the trackless forest was clearly far superior to the islanders', and she was a brave fighter. But would the other islanders agree to set her free?

Her musings were cut short, however, by a string of profanity from Miron. Alarmed, she said, "What's wrong? Is something wrong?"

Miron made a disgusted noise and gestured toward Yin. The robber's spear was stuck embedded in the dinosaur's left eye socket. Sparks and fizzing noises emanated from the thing.

"Oh, shoot," Maya said, walking over to inspect the damage. "This doesn't look good."

Miron, fiddling with his memex, growled, "He's not responding. That spear must've hit something vital."

The others gathered around.

"I guess that's the end of my free ride, huh?" Aiko said, pulling a wry face.

"Hang on a little longer," Miron muttered, tapping at the memex. "Let me see if there's anything I can..."

They waited for several minutes, but Yin remained motionless. Finally, Miron gave up, and shrugged at his companions. "I might be able to fix him if I had decent facilities, but as it is..." He shook his head. "Sorry, people."

"Not your fault," Maya said, patting him on the shoulder.

"Well, it was a good thing while it lasted," Jame said. "Let's unload him. Aiko, how about if we make some crutches for you?"

"Even with crutches, she won't be able to keep up with the rest of us," Carla said. "Not yet, anyway. We're going to have to put her back on the stretcher."

They remade the stretcher, using the travois poles, and were soon on their way once more.

Thanks to the mental training she had received while working with the Monitors of Eil Malk, Maya had a good working knowledge of techniques to survive in the wild, but it wasn't up to Blue Petal's lifetime of experience in and around the Blue Ridge forests of North Carolina. Maya would have to think for a moment to identify a tree or a shrub, whereas if asked, Blue Petal knew them immediately.

Even so, Maya had a complete survivalist background thanks to the coded molecules that had been spliced into her DNA, though she had never gone camping or backpacking before this expedition.

THEY MADE GOOD PROGRESS for several days, during which time Aiko exercised religiously in order to regain her ability to walk. They made crutches for her, and although their use slowed the party down somewhat, she refused to be carried anymore. It was Aiko's insistence on moving under her own steam, and her propensity for exercise, that finally led to Maya's realization of the Asian woman's true identity.

One morning, shortly after they had broken their fast and before they started packing up to get back on the road once more, Maya was taking a short walk away from the camp, organizing her thoughts, when she came upon Aiko doing yoga asanas in a small clearing. Not wanting to disturb her, Maya watched while Aiko moved smoothly from one pose to another, always pausing in between, and finally ending face down in what Maya knew from her own experiments with yoga to be the child position: sitting back on the knees, with arms extended out flat on the ground as if making obeisance.

Then it clicked: Maya knew who Aiko was.

Her sharp intake of breath alerted Aiko, and the Asian woman came slowly out of the posture and smiled at her. "Hellay, Maya."

"Hellay, Drusilla."

Aiko smiled. She did not appear at all put out. "I was wondering how long it would take you to figure that out."

"I feel kind of silly that I didn't before this. Where's your mole?" She was referring to the small mole beneath Drusilla's lower lip, to the left of her chin. "It was a charming little imperfection."

"Oh, I covered it with some makeup," the girl said.

"I would have recognized you lots sooner if you'd left it alone."

"I know."

Maya sat on the ground near Aiko's yoga mat. "Why even bother?" Then she nodded. "I bet you didn't want to be unmasked as one of the Oracles of Time." The Oracles were from the far future and appeared in the guise of young children. She still wasn't clear on what, exactly, the Oracles' purpose was, but the easiest answer seemed to be that they guarded the space-time continuum from tampering by outside influences.

"Something like that," Aiko said.

"Why are you even here in the first place?" Maya said. "I mean, I think I have a pretty good handle on what's going on. I admit we didn't expect to be marooned like this, but I doubt you did, either."

"You're right. I didn't. But I'm glad I'm here to help. Which I would have been able to do a better job of, had I not sustained a broken bone. But I'm healing quickly, and I can actually speed things along a bit. I didn't want the Doc to get suspicious, though, because I would heal faster than a normal person. Also, we, the other Oracles and I, have observed that you have lost some focus. We want you to do a better job of being in the moment."

"I've been kind of busy," said Maya, not bothering to hide her sarcasm.

Aiko took no notice. "Understood, but I'd like to start working with you on a daily basis. Meditation and yoga. These will help you regain your equanimity. This journey we are on is stressful, and you will need all the assistance you can get."

Maya sighed. "I guess I have lost sight of that," she said. "All of it seems so meaningless. The stars..." She gestured up at the sky. "They, they are so far beyond us. I can't help seeing our existence here as trivial. What's the point of it all?

"*Survival* is the point," Aiko said. "Yours, mine, even Gabriel's. I have been unable to hunt for food for us, but I am going to push my healing a little so that I can start providing again."

"I don't want you to do that if it's going to have a negative effect on your health," Maya said. "I can't allow it. We've already lost Priscilla. We have a long way to go before we're safe back in Greensboro."

Aiko was nodding. "Which is all the more reason why I have to start contributing my share of the work. Tomorrow, in fact, I *am* going to start."

Maya scoffed. "Yeah, well, Carla may have something to say about that."

"Don't worry about Carla," Aiko replied. She smiled. "I can be very... persuasive. And in the meantime, please keep my little secret to yourself, okay? I would rather not have to go into a long explanation of my true identity."

"All right; I promise."

"Good. Now: let's meditate for a little while, all right?"

"Yes." Fifteen minutes later, after doing her best to keep her mind blank and her senses open, Maya opened her eyes, and realized she knew what to do about Blue Petal.

When they had returned to the others, she called everyone together. "I propose that we release Blue Petal."

The young warrior woman blinked at her in surprise.

"What?" Miron yelped. "But..." He stopped.

"If we don't have Yin to help us, I'd think we should keep Blue Petal. She's useful," Jame said.

"Well, that's part of why I think we should release her," said Maya. "Blue basically saved our skins when the Bear Clan attacked us."

"She started the festivities when she shot that one guy," Carla said, rather sourly. "They might have passed by without noticing us."

"They saw Yin, though," Aiko pointed out. "They knew something was up. They wouldn't have gone farther without checking the area."

"I think Aiko's right," Jame said. "Blue Petal reduced the odds against us. Okay, I'm with Maya: let's let her go."

The discussion went on for many minutes. Blue Petal sat, impassive all the while, listening.

At the end of it they had achieved consensus. Maya raised her hand. "Blue Petal. Thank you for assisting us. We're not going to keep you any longer. Feel free to leave anytime."

Blue Petal inclined her head in acknowledgement, and said, "Thank you, friends. I'm sorry that we started of badly, but I have come to see that you are honorable people, and I am pleased that I could be of assistance. I also appreciate your trust. With your permission, I will stay with you a while longer. If we continue on this road, tomorrow we will pass the place marking the farthest I have ever been from my home territory. I'm curious about that, so I'd like to continue."

"We're pleased to have you," Maya said, and extended her hand. Blue Petal gripped it, and went around to the others, shaking their hands in turn.

"We'll give you some food and water," Maya said as Blue Petal prepared to take her leave.

"You've little enough to spare," she replied. She lifted her crossbow. "I have this; it's all I will need. There is water aplenty."

Maya nodded, knowing this to be true: they had passed a number of streams along the way. "Then farewell, and good fortune to you."

"Thank you." Without another word, Blue Petal walked away, toward the west.

They watched her go until a turn in the road hid her from their sight. Then they set out in the opposite direction.

MAYA THOUGHT ABOUT Blue Petal throughout the morning and wished the young warrior woman had stayed with them a little longer. She also missed Yin, but more for his strength and ability to throw a scare into potential attackers than because he had any personality worth the word.

The company was rather subdued. Everyone seemed occupied with his or her own thoughts, and there was little talking. When they stopped for lunch, Maya sought out Aiko and walked with her a few hundred yards down the road.

"Something is troubling you," Maya said without preamble. "What might that be?"

"I didn't realize it was so obvious," the Asian woman said, frowning.

"It probably isn't, to anyone else." She tapped her forehead. "But I've had the benefit of training by your Oracles; it's made me more empathic."

Aiko nodded slowly. "Yes, I should have realized that. Very well. There is indeed something on my mind." She chewed her lips for a moment. "Now, you know that we have explained to you that the stars in our local group—in fact, the majority of stars in the galaxy—are intelligent, and communicate via fluctuating neutrino emissions, over hundreds and thousands and even millions of years, and as many light-years of distance."

Maya nodded, gesturing for Aiko to continue.

"And we, the Oracles, are extensions, if you will, of this solar system's sun."

Maya nodded again, more slowly. "I suspected as much," she said. "Are there Oracles like you on other inhabited worlds?"

"Yes. Intelligent life is a relatively rare commodity throughout the galaxy, however. There are only a few dozen intelligent civilizations in the galaxy, and I can tell you that none of them have encountered any of the others." She paused. "However... there is a rather serious problem that we have discovered."

"Oh? And what is that?"

"We have learned that we have counterparts, if you will, among what we call 'rogue stars.' These are stars, usually found isolated in small clusters, that share chemical signatures of rare elements that seem to have had a deleterious impact on their thinking processes. They have formed a community of their own, with values antithetical to ours. We promote civilization where we find it, watching over it and doing what we can to prevent it from destroying itself and any neighboring ones. We engage in discussions meant to raise our awareness of time and space and life. The rogues, however, actively seek to subvert our society and cleanse the galaxy of what they call 'the scourge of planet-based life.'"

"Well, that doesn't sound good at all," Maya said. Having some understanding of how powerful the star-minds were, the thought of "evil" ones made her uneasy. "Is there one such cluster nearby?"

"The nearest one is the Hyades Cluster," said Aiko, "which appears in the constellation Taurus."

Maya nodded. During her university career, she had been a professor of astronomy. She knew the Hyades Cluster was about 150 light-years away from Earth, which was, as she had come to understand, uncomfortably close.

In fact... "Have they had any communication with people here on Earth?"

"Ah. You have caught on very quickly," Aiko said. "It's possible that representatives of the cluster have appeared on Earth in the past, seeking to influence events."

Several thoughts flashed through Maya's mind all at once. If the denizens of that star cluster were that close to Earth, it was conceivable that they had had contact with Earth people any number of times since the beginning of history. Was it possible that they had been responsible, directly or indirectly, for the mad decisions that had brought about the tragedy of 2173 that had almost wiped out the human race?

When she brought up the later point to Aiko, the Asian woman looked grim. "That is our fear," she said. "If it's true, then the rogues came very close indeed to wiping out all life on this world. They are bound to try it again."

"Wait a minute," Maya said. "You appear to us as human beings. I remember thinking once that you were like projections. Solid, three-dimensional, but... I don't know, like old-time holograms or something, but made of flesh."

"That's a good description of us."

"Okay, then, does that mean that the rogues can do that trick, too? That they could appear here, on Earth, looking like regular, everyday people?"

"That's exactly what it means," Aiko said. "They have personifications like us."

"Have you ever met any?"

"No, not to my knowledge."

"So... you can't track them? Do you know where they are at any given time?"

"No. I wish we did. I don't even know if any are on Earth at the present time. I'm sure there are, though."

Maya thought hard for a few moments. *The problem here is, I have no way to tell if Aiko and her fellow Oracles aren't the rogues! I mean, I don't think they are, but—how would I ever know? How could I prove it one way or the other? I just have her word that they're the good guys.*

She pondered this problem for the rest of the day, barely noticing the country through which they passed.

Route 40, the former highway they were following, had in previous times been a four-lane road: two going east, two going west, with a metal divider fence between them and on either side, to prevent automobiles from going off the road. The fencing had rusted away, and the road was occasionally difficult to find, but the broken pavement underfoot helped keep them on the path, as did the fact that the road was elevated from the surrounding land. The going was hard on Aiko at times, but they still had the stretcher with which they could assist her over the really rough spots.

Maya said nothing to the others about her conversation with the Oracle. The more she thought about it, the more certain she became that one of the Rogues, at least, had to be somewhere on Earth. Given that Eil Malk and the other islands were one of the seats of the slowly regrowing civilization, it seemed logical to her to assume that a Rogue would be present, observing and reporting back to its fellows. From what Aiko had told her, the Rogues wouldn't be satisfied to have *nearly* wrecked Earth—they'd want to finish the job.

It depends on a few factors, she said to herself. *Are they really watching? If they are here, do they know about us? There must be other pockets of technological development on Earth... what if the Rogues are there instead of here? How many Rogues are we talking about? There were half a dozen Oracles. There could easily be that many Rogues.*

She wished she could talk to her brother, Ahmed. He would certainly be interested in learning about the Rogues. She had told him about the Oracles, and he had been skeptical, but her former tutor, Saravati, also a Monitor like Ahmed, had vouched for the truth of Maya's claims. As far as she knew, however, Ahm had had no direct contact with any of the Oracles.

She wondered if Saravati had; and resolved to ask Aiko about it.

So lost was she in her thoughts that when Jame tapped her shoulder, she winced.

"Did you hear me?" he asked, grinning.

"Uhm, no, sorry. I was thinking."

"Yeah, I thought I smelled rubber bands burning. Listen, I was asking about Aiko. She seems to be a lot better. She's walking more easily. I don't think she'll need her crutches before very long."

"Oh? Uh, I hadn't noticed." She glanced over shoulder. Miron and Carla were currently walking with Aiko to keep her company, freeing Jame for another half hour or so until he took his turn beside her.

"Well, it's true. Don't you think it's a little, I don't know, *off* that she is healing so quickly?"

Shoot. He was on to something. Don't want to make him more suspicious... She kept her tone deliberately light, and said, in an offhand a manner, "Well, you know, some people heal faster than others."

He scoffed. "Healing is one thing; the woman has a broken leg!"

"I don't know; what do you want me to say?" She projected some irritation into her tone. "Ask Carla about it; she's the doctor, not me."

"All right, all right, relax. It's just a question. But I'll check with Carla, as you say."

"Good. Look, Jame—I'm sorry. I have a lot on my mind. This whole situation is so far out of my experience... the aerostat crash, then having to walk nearly three hundred kilometers back to Greensboro... it's a lot."

"You're right, I know. But we've made good time, even factoring Aiko's leg into the situation." He sighed. "I wish we'd been able to hang onto Yin. He was a good addition to the team."

"Yeah... I agree. Having to take turns again lugging Aiko's stretcher was slowing us down, so if she can keep up with the crutches. So much the better. And as you say, she's healing quickly, so maybe she'll be able to walk without them soon."

"I still say, that's awfully fast."

This time Maya simply shrugged and said nothing.

Chapter Five - A Pleasant Surprise

Two more days passed as they slogged along. No one attacked them. In fact, the countryside seemed oddly deserted, though certainly not lifeless. Occasionally a deer bounded across their path, and once Aiko, who was always watching and ready, brought down a young doe with her bow.

"Ha ha!" she exulted. "All right, *now* I feel like I'm contributing something."

She butchered the deer, with Miron's rather squeamish assistance, and packed up the meat as best she could.

"We can't take time to smoke it," she said, "but it'll keep for a few days with our cold packs." These were renewable and required only some sun to power their cooling units. They were no substitute for a real refrigerator, but they were useful for camping.

They were by now more than halfway to their goal and were approaching the outskirts of a town Gabriel said had once been called Statesville. The roadway continued in its decayed condition, and Maya paid it no mind until Carla whistled for attention.

Maya looked around. "What's—uh, what is it, Doc?"

"Look there," she said, pointing to a crooked metal sign, much eaten with rust. "If I'm not mistaken, that sign says there's a hospital nearby. I would love the opportunity to see if I can get some supplies."

Jame made a face. "After all this time, there's not likely to be much left to scavenge," he said.

"I know, but still."

"Worth a try, maybe," Maya said. "Miron? Ask Gabriel to check his map files and see if there's a hospital around here."

"There is," said the AI a moment later. "Here's what I found. Davis Regional Medical Center."

Maya examined the screen. "Well, it's only a few hundred meters off the road, here," she said. "Pretty close." She squinted in the direction Gabriel indicated the hospital should be. "Is that it? I think I see some ruins through the trees."

"That would be it," Gabriel replied.

Maya took a deep breath, then blew it out. "Very well. It's close enough that we won't be wasting much time to investigate," she said. "Let's do it."

"Be wary of snakes," Gabriel said as they moved off to their left, off the road. "This is copperhead country."

"Copperhead?" Miron asked.

"Yes," said Gabriel. "The eastern copperhead, *Agkistrodon contortrix*. A venomous pit viper species, with dark brown hourglass-shaped markings overlaid on a light reddish brown or brown gray background."

"And venomous, you say," Carla said as she picked her way through the underbrush in Miron's tracks.

"Mildly," Gabriel said. "Unlikely to kill, but the bite can be painful."

"Hmph."

The medical center had fallen into complete ruin, however, and there was nothing useful to be salvaged there, to the Doctor's disappointment.

"Oh, well," she said as they made their way back to Route 40 after spending a fruitless hour exploring the tumbled stones and the few smashed, rusty machines remaining in the buildings. "Thanks for indulging me, anyway."

As they were leaving the campus, which for the most part more closely resembled a second-growth forest, Aiko suddenly snapped, "Stop! Everyone, freeze."

Aiko wasn't given to jokes, so they immediately halted. A mockingbird called from a nearby tree as wind soughed through the branches.

"What is it?" Maya whispered after a few moments.

"I saw something move over there," Aiko said. She had nocked an arrow and pointed with it off to their left.

Tensely, Maya scanned the trees in that direction. "I don't see anything," she murmured.

"Just... just don't move."

"There!" Jame said, pointing a few degrees left of where Aiko had indicated.

Maya saw a brown, four-legged body flash through the undergrowth at the far end of what had probably once been a parking area. There was only one badly rusted car sitting there now, with weeds and saplings sprouting from its engine compartment.

"What is it?" she asked.

Aiko shook her head. "If I see it again, I'll try to get a shot at it," she said.

But the creature, whatever it was, didn't show itself.

After a few anxious minutes, the band got under way once more and were soon back on main road. Unnerved, they moved faster than usual. Everyone wanted to get away from the place where they had had a scare.

"What do you think it was?" Maya asked, dropping back to walk with Aiko as she stumped along on her crutches, with her bow and arrows slung across her back.

"Not sure. I *think* it was a dog. Definitely wasn't a bear, or any kind of cat... don't know what else it could have been." She shrugged. "Maybe a big raccoon, or something."

"Okay," Maya said. "We'll keep an eye out. I don't know what else we can do."

By the time they stopped for the night and lit a fire for cooking, the medical complex, and whatever animal lurked there, was kilometers behind them.

Conversation was somewhat muted that evening. They ate their supper—a delicious venison stew augmented with wild vegetables, concocted by Carla—and lounged around the fire telling stories and joking.

At one point Maya looked up and saw a pair of green eyes gleaming at her out of the darkness. She exclaimed and got to her feet, legs apart, laser pistol at the ready.

"What is it?" Jame asked, alarmed.

She shook her head. "All I saw were eyes."

Aiko blew out a breath. "How big? Could you tell?"

"I don't know. Fairly big. Bigger than a skunk or a possum, I think."

Miron stepped up beside her. "Think it's whatever Aiko spotted at the med center, following us?"

"I doubt it. That was hours ago. Wouldn't we have seen it on our trail?"

He shrugged. "How often do we look back? And if it was an animal, it was probably slinking along in the foliage. I mean, if it was really following us. Whatever you saw just now, that might be a local boy."

"Maybe."

She took the first watch, which was supposed to be Jame's. "I'm a little edgy," she said. "I'll wake you in a couple-three hours."

"Thanks, I don't mind getting a little extra sleep."

She flashed him a smile. "I didn't think you would."

Jame turned in, along with the others. Maya sat by the crackling fire, feeding it some wood every so often. She repeatedly scanned the area, but the eyes didn't show up again.

There were, however, plenty of insects filling the night with their trilling and buzzing, and flying around the fire, getting in her face. Mosquitoes didn't bother them because before the expedition left Eil Malk, its members had had universal vaccinations meant to stave off any diseases—and a slight tweak of their genetic structure to render their blood unpalatable to biting bugs. It was, she reflected, one of the benefits of modern life.

The night was so peaceful and quiet that she had the time to think about some things that had been in the back of her mind.,

Her relationship to Jame, for one. Over the past year, since the crisis with Peleliu that had ended with Eil Malk's former nemesis joining with it as an ally, she and Jame had become lovers. She was happy with the way things were going. He was smart, good-looking, sexy, and had the knack of making her laugh—no easy task, as she knew her siblings would say. She had always been the serious one, even more so than Ahmed.

She closed her eyes for a moment—and fell asleep. She jerked awake a moment later and looked around to make sure no-one had seen her lapse. Embarrassed, and relieved that she hadn't been observed, she poked at the fire with a stick, stirring it up, then leaned over to grab another small log to feed it.

She saw a pair of green eyes staring at her just beyond the reach of the fire's illumination. She scrambled to her feet with a cry. The eyes vanished.

Jame sorted and propped himself up on his elbows. "Hum? Time f'r me to take over, babe?"

"Uhm, no. No. Go back to sleep. You have another half hour."

"'kay." Jame burrowed back into his bedroll.

There was no question now that Maya was going to drop off to sleep again, not after seeing those eyes. The minutes ticked slowly by until it was at last time to rouse Jame for his turn at watch.

"Hellay," he said blearily when she shook his shoulder. He climbed to his feet, stretched, farted, and leaned over to give her a kiss.

"You smell," she said, fondly.

"It's the venison," he said.

"Sure."

"Find a scapegoat, I always say. Hey, didn't you wake me up a little while ago?'

"Um, yes, well—sort of."

"Sort of?" You did or you didn't. Come on."

"All right, yes, I did. I saw the eyes again."

He was immediately alert. "You did? Where?"

She gestured to the north. "That way."

"Okay, thanks for the heads-up. I'll be on the look-out."

"Good. I mean, I don't think it's anything, really, but..."

"Yeah." He kissed her again. "Look, I'm on it—get some sleep. You look like you need it."

"Yeah, I really do."

She wrapped herself up in her bedclothes and closed her eyes. She had feared that the jolt supplied by the watching green eyes would keep her awake, but she was asleep almost at once, and stayed that way for the rest of the night.

The next morning, she was annoyed that no one had woke her up for her second turn standing watch, but Jame said, "Well, I told Miron about the eyes you saw, and asked him to tell Carla when it was her turn, and we agreed that you should just sleep through for once."

She playfully punched his shoulder. "Not good," she said, but she was rather glad he had, because now she felt rested. Her concern about the unknown watcher seemed much less serious in the light of day, especially after a good breakfast.

The morning was cool with a hint of rain in the air, but precipitation held off and the sun came out after they had been walking for a few hours, lightening everyone's mood.

Maya had shared her experience in the night with Aiko, who looked serious. "I think something's on our trail," she said. "Well, it's probably nothing serious; nothing to worry about. Maybe just some curious forest critter. After all, I bet there haven't been all that many people around her for years and years."

"You think?" Miron asked, walking at her side. Today was the first day Aiko was trying to walk without her crutches. She was slow, but otherwise had no real difficulties. Maya caught the Doc casting puzzled glances at the Asian woman throughout the day and tried to keep her amusement under wraps. *If you knew she was an Oracle, I wonder what you'd say?* Maya grinned at the thought. *I'll probably have to tell them all one of these days, though.* She resolved to speak with Aiko at the first opportunity about unmasking her. She didn't want to reveal the woman's secret without making sure she wouldn't object.

For the rest of the day they made fairly good time. The sun was beginning to set when they came to place where the road wound through a narrow valley in the hills, really no more than a steep-sided notch, with vertical rock walls on either side. They were about halfway through this when four dogs appeared ahead of them, snarling.

"Hold up!" Maya snapped. Everyone halted. "Okay, let's back away, real slow," she said quietly. "I don't want to get into a fight. We'll wait for them to—"

"Maya," Aiko said softly.

Yeah," Maya replied absently without looking at her.

"Behind us."

Over her shoulder, Maya saw that four more dogs had appeared, blocking their retreat.

"Aw, balls." A drop of perspiration rolled down her forehead. "Aiko?"

"Here," said the Asian. She took a stance and prepared to shoot the biggest dog ahead of them.

"I'll take the ones in the back," Jame said, taking his laser pistol out of its holster.

The odds aren't good, Maya said to herself as she took aim on one of their canine attackers. The dogs weren't all of one breed, she saw.

Aiko launched an arrow toward the dogs blocking them in front. The animals flinched back, almost as if they knew what it was. Maya noticed that the dogs that had trapped them from the rear were also keeping their distance.

"Good," she said through clenched jaws. "You know what a gun is, I see. Hold that thought, doggies."

She raised her gun—and then the biggest of the dogs, a sheepdog from the look of it, stepped forward. "No!" It said in a gruff voice.

Maya blinked. "What? Did you... *say* something?"

It growled, and said, "Said... *no*."

"Holy..." breathed Miron. His jaw hung open in amazement. "Is that thing *talking*?"

"I... talk," said the sheepdog, and came a step closer. "I hold dogs 'ack. You say who you are, where going."

You have got to be kidding me, Maya thought. *But okay... I'm game.* She licked her lips and cleared her throat. "I am Maya Komarov," she said, as calmly as she could manage. "These are my companions: Miron, Jame, Aiko, and Carla. The aircraft we were in crashed, and we have been forced to travel on foot back to Greensboro."

The dogs growled, whined, and yipped among themselves for a few moments.

"Do you understand me?" Maya asked.

"Yes," said the sheepdog. "I...p...p...Pax." It had obvious trouble with the "p" sound. Maya thought she knew why: the dog had no lips, and certain plosives like p and b would be hard for a lipless creature to form. F, m, v, and w would probably also be difficult for it.

"Pax," she repeated.

"Yes." It indicated the other dogs with an inclination of its head. "These... co'rades."

"Comrades?"

"Yes. This our territory. You not welcome here."

Welcome, he must mean, but he can't make a good 'm' sound. "Please tell your comrades that we mean no harm. All we want is to pass through and be on our way."

"Can the other dogs, your comrades, can they speak?" Miron asked, stepping forward.

"Nnno," Pax said, not meeting their eyes. "I only."

To Carla, Maya murmured, "Do we have any venison left?"

"Yeah—why do you ask?"

"I want to give Pax and his buddies a treat," Maya replied.

"Treeeet?" Pax asked. He began to drool.

Carla rummaged in her pack and brought out a wrapped parcel. "It's kind of getting old," she said, handing it to Maya.

"Dogs won't care," Maya said. She unwrapped the meat, then crouched down and placed it on the ground. "Please accept this offering," she said, "as a token of our peaceful intentions."

Pax yipped to the other dogs. To Maya, he said, "We check. If poison, you die."

Maya pursed her lips. "It's not contaminated, just a little old. We killed the deer a few days ago."

One dog, a Jack Russell terrier, came forward and sniffed at the meat. He barked at Pax, who bent his head down and took a piece of the venison.

There was not enough of the meat for all eight dogs to have a very big piece, but they nevertheless shared it among themselves. After Pax took his share, the others came forward, one at a time, for theirs.

"We thank," said Pax.

"A dog of few words," Jame said softly.

"I don't think speaking our language is high on their list of priorities," Maya said, smiling.

Pax evidently heard this, for he showed his teeth in a doggy grin. "Is good," he said. "The 'eat."

"The meat, yes," Maya said. "We're pleased you like it. Look, Pax, it's going to be dark soon. We would like your permission to camp here for the night. We'll leave in the morning and will trouble you no more."

"We allow," said the sheepdog. "Don't hate you but need to take care. There are those... who hunt us."

Maya nodded. "such as the Bear Clan, maybe?"

Pax growled deep in his throat. "They have taken young," he said. "We hate."

"Good guess," Carla murmured.

"You... hollow," Pax said. "Take to 'lace to rest."

"Follow?" Maya asked.

"Yes. Hollow." He turned and walked off. The humans, after shrugging at each other, followed him.

Maya walked beside Aiko. "What do you think?" she asked the disguised Oracle.

"It's safe," Aiko said without hesitating. "I don't know how it is that he can talk, but it's clear that he and his fellows are extremely intelligent, more so than most dogs. There's a story there."

"No doubt."

Pax and his canine crew led them a kilometer or two down the road, then off into the undergrowth along what Maya would have called a game path, until they arrived at a clearing. Here a number of other dogs, mostly females, were playing with some puppies. There were a four other sheepdogs among them. As soon as they saw the humans their hackles rose, and they began growling until Pax silenced them with a series of barks and yips.

One young male, a German Shepherd, who was among the females—as a companion or a guard Maya could not judge—barked at

Pax and snarled, as did a couple of the other canines. Pax returned the snarl with interest. The younger male subsided, as did the other dogs, but his hackles remained raised.

"Interesting," Aiko said. "Seems to be a dominance issue."

"I can understand that with another male, but what about the females?"

Aiko shook her head. "I don't know. I suppose there are factions among the pack. I'm sure that that male is going to challenge Pax one of these days."

Maya wrinkled her nose. "Hopefully not until after we leave."

Later, after they had built a fire and were preparing the evening meal, Maya and her companions were surprised when most of the dogs came and lay about the campsite, tongues lolling out.

Pax sat by Maya. "Um, may I pet you?" she asked. "I mean, I like dogs. We had a dog when I was a little girl."

Pax inclined his head without saying anything. Maya reached out and tentatively stroked him. He closed his eyes.

Good doggy, she wanted to say, but restrained herself, not being sure how he'd take it.

The other people likewise showed some affection to the dogs nearest them. For the first time in many days, Maya felt safe. *How could I not, with all these dogs around?*

"So, Pax," she said, stretching her legs out before her, "tell me about yourself. For example, how did you learn to talk?"

Because of Pax's relatively clumsy speech, the story took a long time for the dog to tell. The other sheepdogs in the pack were his siblings, two brothers and two sisters, born in the same litter of puppies. They were more intelligent than the other dogs, but not as smart as Pax—and none of them could speak.

Pax, and his brothers and sisters, were the result of genetic experiments conducted by a human couple, Christopher and Dianne

Schank. For some unknown reason, Pax was able to learn how to speak, after a fashion.

As he put it, with his tail between his legs, "I not quite dog, not quite 'uman."

Although she could not read his emotions, Maya couldn't help feeling sorry for him. He didn't really belong to either species and he knew it.

The pups were raised, isolated from other dogs, by the Schanks, who used sophisticated gene-splicing techniques and microsurgery to create a group of "super dogs." Pax and his siblings, who were now three years old, had passed a happy and peaceful puppyhood, with the Schanks focusing most of their attention on Pax as it became clear that his level of intelligence was roughly equivalent to that of a twelve- or thirteen-year-old human.

Educating the dog was an erratic and frustrating process for both canines and humans. Pax had a good command of spoken English but could not communicate well because his dog larynx could not duplicate some human phonemes, and because his mouth was not the right shape. He could read, though he was unable to write because he lacked the ability to hold a pen or pencil. He could type on a computer keyboard altered for his paws, but only at a painfully slow rate.

Miron had been listening while Pax spoke. Now he said, "I wonder if I could get Gabriel to work up a translation application."

Maya looked at him in surprise. "How would that work?"

"Well, we question Pax; get a sample of his speech, everything he can say. Gabriel could then be able to translate his currently crude speech into proper English. It would be easier for him, because he could speak more quickly if he didn't have to be so careful. And it would make it easier for us to understand him."

"Okay," said Maya. "That sounds like a plan. How long do you think it would take?"

"What do you think, Gabriel?" Miron asked the AI.

"I estimate a day or two," was the reply.

Maya turned to the dog. "Would you be willing to stay with us for a couple of days?" she asked.

"Wait, hold up," Jame said. "What would be the point? No offense, Pax, but we won't be staying here; we've got to get to Greensboro."

The dog replied that he been thinking about that and had a proposition for them.

"I save until can talk 'etter," he said.

"Talk better?" Maya asked. Pax nodded. Maya looked around at the other people. "Well, what say you?" she asked. "Shall we take a couple of days off from the road? That would give Aiko a chance to heal more fully. And there's also your arm, Carla, where you were shot."

The suggestion was adopted. Although the humans had every intention of getting back to their fellows in Greensboro, they all agreed that a break wasn't a bad idea. Miron and the dogs got down to the task of working up a translation program for Pax's imperfect speech.

SOONER THAN ANYONE expected, the AI announced success. And sure enough, a short demonstration proved to be impressive.

His raw speech was as imperfect as ever, and larded with growling and whining, but Gabriel's program rendered it clearly. "I have not had any interactions with a computer like this," said Pax through the AI's program.

"That's amazing," Maya said with a grin, and the other humans nodded in agreement.

Pax, listening to the output, wagged his tail. "Now then," he went on, "I can tell you about my idea." He went on to explain that the Schanks had raised him and his siblings in a well-protected compound not far from where he and his pack had first encountered the islanders.

"You see," he said, "there were bands of marauders in the region, robbing people and killing or enslaving them."

"We have had some experience with that sort of thing," Maya said, and told him about the Bear Clan.

"Yes, we have heard of them." Pax said. "But there are others who are worse. We knew that some of them were aware of the compound, but we assumed it was secure and well enough protected that we would be safe." He paused. "We were wrong."

Then a large band of the thieves managed to breach the enclosure's walls. They smashed much of the Schanks' equipment and took them hostage.

"My siblings and I managed to escape. I don't think they knew we were different from other dogs. Since that day, nearly a year ago, we have been watching the marauders and trying to come up with a plan to defeat them and rescue our parents."

Jame looked askance at Maya. "Their... parents."

Maya glared at him. Turning to the dog, she said, "I take that to mean you know where they are being held."

"Yes. And I would like to propose a deal. If you will help us rescue the Schanks, I will accompany you to Greensboro."

He barked at the other dogs, who barked back. "They concur," Pax said. "My brother, Jaxon, will act as interim leader while I am gone."

"Pax, excuse us for a few minutes while we talk this over," Maya said. She took the other humans aside. "Well? What say you?"

Jame said, "I can see the benefit of having Pax along. He'd make a great lookout. But that means we'd have to agree to help him rescue his owners." He made a face. "So, we'd be going up against a bunch of bad guys, armed with who knows what."

"Yeah, I don't like it," Carla said. "I think it's too risky. It's not really our battle." The others murmured their assent.

Maya nodded. "Okay, understandable. But let's get Pax in on the discussion. Maybe he can give us some additional insight." She motioned for the dog to join them and explained to him their reluctance.

"I cannot blame you," he said through the AI. "However, our parents' stronghold contains a large store of weapons and food. I will give you some if you help us. In addition, the robbers have food and weapons, too. You. can keep as much of that as you want, if we are successful."

"How much do they have?" Jame asked.

"I am not sure, but we have watched the compound, and have seen them carrying large boxes that we know contain guns, ammunition, and food."

"How do you know what's in those boxes?" Miron asked.

"We can smell them," was the simple reply.

Miron nodded thoughtfully. "Gabriel? Can you tell me how sensitive a dog's sense of smell is?"

"Estimates vary," said the AI, "But most experts agree that a dog's sense of smell is between ten thousand and a hundred thousand times better than that of a human."

Maya and the others were silent for a moment. "Well, now," she said at last. "I guess if he says they can smell that stuff, he knows what he's talking about."

"The only problem with that is we can only carry so many additional supplies," Aiko said. "I hate to say this, but I really won't be able to carry much more than I already am."

"Right; your leg. Well, we'll figure something out."

Pax, overhearing this exchange, turned to the other dogs and barked at them. A conversation of sorts ensured for the next few minutes. Then Pax turned to Maya.

"Jaxon and I can carry some things, if you can rig panniers for us."

Miron turned to Maya. *Panniers?* he mouthed.

"Carriers, you know—like on cykes. Baskets or bags over the back wheel. Like saddlebags."

"Oh."

"We could manage four or six kilograms, I believe," Pax added.

Maya nodded slowly. "Okay, well, that would help. Ok, folks, what do we think?"

Her comrades looked at each other and shrugged. Aiko said, "I think I want to know more about the layout of this redoubt or whatever it is, where these robbers are holed up."

They spent some time peppering Pax and, by extension, the other dogs, with questions. A view of the hideout gradually emerged. Apparently it covered about three acres inside a chain-link fence topped with razor wire. Inside the fence was a large two-story house with a cement block outbuilding and a barn. Ten or eleven brigands lived there, preying on nearby communities and passing travelers, as well as hunting and fishing.

"Are we really sure we want to do this?" Jame asked Maya later while they were having lunch.

She frowned. "Look, wouldn't you like to have someone as loyal as Pax on your side if *you* were kidnapped?"

"Well, yes; but we don't even know if the Schanks are even still alive."

"That shouldn't be too hard to learn," Miron said.

"How so?"

Miron shrugged. "Send a couple of the dogs to find out. They should be able to smell them, right?"

Maya put the request to Pax, who readily agreed. "We are so grateful that you are willing to help us," the dog said. "I promise you we will give you all possible assistance."

Chapter Six - Others First

The first step was indeed to ascertain if Christopher and Dianne Schank were still alive. The stronghold was about seven kilometers from their present location. Jame volunteered to accompany Pax and Jaxon on a scouting foray.

The others waited where they were and made friends with the other dogs while they waited. Sticks were thrown and heads scratched. After about three hours, Jame and the dogs returned.

"It's just as they said," Jame reported. "Fenced-in compound, and so on. I'm not sure how we'd get through the fence. We hid in the underbrush and just watched. There's a guard who walks the perimeter. I'm sure they have one posted at night, too. Maybe more than one."

Pax said that he and the other dogs could dig a good-sized hole under the fence in a short time. "There needs to be a diversion," he added, "to give us time to dig."

"All right," Maya said. "First, though, let's go to where the Schanks lived, and see if anything's left there, in terms of weapons, or anything else we could use to provide some distraction."

The dogs agreed. Pax led Maya and Aiko along a circuitous path through a heavily forested region. They came to a clearing in which sat the Schanks' compound. It was surrounded by a tall stone wall with shards of broken glass set into its top. The only entrance was a sturdy steel gate. A keypad on a short metal pole stood beside the gate, which was closed. The dog approached the pad and pushed the keys with his nose. The gate slowly rolled back into a recessed slot.

"Ohhh," said Aiko. "I see. They designed it so that Pax could use it, too."

"Clever," said Maya in admiration. She had taken careful note of the sequence of numbers Pax entered on the pad.

They entered the enclosure. Earlier, Pax had informed them through the AI that there were booby traps scattered around. "You must follow me closely," he warned. "Single file."

Now they walked carefully across the innocuous-looking yard toward a small, Cape Cod-style house in the center of the clearing. The only thing at all unusual about it was the large fenced-in dog yard to one side. There were no dogs in it at present. Aiko scanned the ground as they walked. "I don't see anything," she said. "They've done a great job hiding the traps."

Another key pad stood on its pole next to the front door. Again Pax pushed the keys, and again Maya memorized the pattern. The door unlocked with an audible click. Pax stood in front of the door his tongue lolling out.

Suddenly he began howling, startling the women. "What's wrong?" Maya asked the dog.

"Sad!" he managed to say. "'any 'eneries."

"Do you mean, 'many memories'?" Aiko asked.

"Uh huh, uh huh."

"Poor doggy," Aiko said, crouching down to put her arms around him. Pax did not seem to mind this familiarity, and in fact rubbed his head against her. After a moment, he seemed to have composed himself. "Go in?" he asked.

Maya realized what was expected of her: he had no thumbs, and therefore couldn't turn the doorknob.

"Sorry," she said with a smile, and opened the door.

Inside, the house was dusty but neat. There was no sign of weapons or food, even though the kitchen cabinets and refrigerator were well-stocked.

"How long have they been gone, Pax?" Maya asked.

"'ree unths," he said.

"Three months?"

"Uh-huh."

Aiko was looking around the other rooms. "There's nothing here," she said. "A living room, dining room, and a bedroom. Besides the kitchen and bath, that's it."

Pax padded into the kitchen and sat down in front of a small door that Maya had taken to be a pantry. She opened it, and sure enough: cans and boxes and bottles were stacked on shelves.

She looked questioningly at the dog. He said, "'ush third 'ottle on right on dat shelf." He pointed with his nose.

Maya approached the shelf and pushed the bottle lightly. The entire wall opened on hinges, revealing a stairway down into darkness.

"Wow," said Aiko, peering into the stairwell. She flipped a light switch on the wall. Fluorescents came on above them, lighting the way into a hidden basement. "Cool!" She started down the stairs.

Pax barked sharply. "Don't stet on six stet," he said. "'ooey trat."

"Sixth step is booby-trapped?"

"Uh-huh."

They proceeded down the stairs, at the bottom of which was another door and keypad. Once more Pax used his nose to push the keys, and again Maya took note of the sequence. This door opened, showing that it was five inches thick and made of steel painted to look like wood.

Past it was a short hallway with two doors on either side. Maya and Aiko examined the rooms within. Each one was about the size of the living room upstairs, but instead of couches and chairs, there were racks of weapons, shelves of food, a small well-stocked laboratory, boxes of medical supplies, and several freezers.

Exclaiming in delight, Aiko went through the shelves of weapons. She plucked a stubby gun out of its box. "What's this thing?" she asked, squinting at the label. "Flare pistol. Hm. Interesting." She added it to her collection.

"Is there a generator somewhere, Pax?" Maya asked.

"Uh-huh." He walked to the door at the end of the hall and sat in front of it.

She opened the door. A compact generator hummed within.

"I'm impressed," Aiko said. "What powers it?"

"'mall husion reactor," said the dog.

"*What?* A small *fusion* reactor? Holy snot!"

"The Schanks weren't screwing around were they," said Maya. She turned to Pax. "It's damn lucky the kidnappers didn't find this stash."

Pax replied that nothing, not even torture, could have forced the Schanks to reveal its existence.

A short while later they left the compound with high-powered rifles slung over their shoulders. Aiko carried a cloth bag into which she had stuffed some boxes of ammunition, two .38s, an extra energy pistol, and the flare gun. They also had a couple of backpacks full of food concentrates, and four dogs: Pax, Clyde, Willy, and Dashiell.

"Thanks, Pax," said Maya as they walked through the forest on their way back to the others. "This stuff is a great help."

"But now the *fun* part starts," said Aiko. "We have to rescue Mr. and Mrs. Schank."

Back at the campsite, Maya and Aiko showed off their new acquisitions and described what they had seen in the Schanks' compound.

"Sounds like it would be a perfect base for us," Miron observed when they had finished.

"It would be, maybe, if we were staying around here, and if didn't already belong to the Schanks," Maya said dryly.

"There is that," Miron said, turning red. "Sorry, Pax," he added to the dog.

"What we must do now," said Maya, "is come up with a plan to rescue them."

"I've been thinking about that," said Jame. "And this flare thing you've brought back gives me an idea."

SHORTLY BEFORE MIDNIGHT, Maya and Jame accompanied Pax and the other canines to the compound where the men who had kidnapped the Schanks were holed up. The trip took nearly two hours on foot, in the dark. They didn't dare use flashlights after the first three kilometers. Pax said that the kidnappers occasionally patrolled the woods, but that his nose could give them ample warning of anyone approaching their little band.

They had gone over Jame's plan several times, refining it and making sure everyone knew their role. By the time the long walk to the kidnappers' redoubt was completed, everyone was tired, but wide awake and alert. They gathered in a knot near the wire fence.

"Well, with that razor wire, we certainly can't go over it," Maya said. Pax had assured them that the fence was not electrified, but even so, Maya touched it only gingerly. Sure enough, there was no shock, no sparks.

"So far, so good," she murmured. The group spread out to begin their assigned tasks.

It was a simple plan: the dogs would set to work digging *under* the fence in two places across the compound from each other, with Maya and Jame deputized to help one group each.

The dogs did their work efficiently and quickly. Twice guards came by on their usual patrol, forcing the teams to cease their work. Then, armed with short shovels, the humans enlarged the holes. These tasks completed, everyone regrouped at Maya's station and took a few minutes to rest.

Maya looked around at the dogs, and Jame. "Now, we're all clear on what we need to do?"

Jame nodded, and the dogs each gave a quiet affirmative bark.

"Then here we go," Maya said. "And everyone—be careful. There's not much cover between here and the house."

The energy pistol had a stun setting, so Maya, who was a better shot than Jame, commandeered it. She had never shot anyone before, or even stunned them, but she knew she could manage it if she had to.

And she was sure she would have to.

The teams went into the fenced-in area through their two points of entry. While she was squirming through the crude tunnel excavated by the dogs, Maya had time to regret the loss of Yin the dino-bot. *He'd certainly make a hell of a diversion,* she thought. *Well, we'll just have to rely on Jame's idea.*

At this hour, they were sure the robbers would be asleep. Maya and Jame would have to rely on the sensitive noses of the dogs to lead them to where the Schanks were imprisoned, and to alert them if they were about to be discovered by the bad guys.

She looked up at the sky. There were no clouds, and she could tell by the stars that it was just about time for the net part of their plan.

Sure enough, a spout of flame erupted from across the compound, arcing up into the sky, where it burst, showering sparks while a glowing ball slowly floated toward the ground: Jame had fired the flare gun.

At the same moment, the dogs began barking furiously, from points opposite the two tunnels. Lights came on in the house, along with a string of obscenities.

The front door opened and two men carrying rifles burst out. Aiming carefully, Maya shot them with the stun gun. They dropped in their tracks.

Decent, she said to herself, grinning, and began moving toward the house.

"Max? Leroy?" someone called from inside. "What the hell is going on out there?"

There was more shouting, more indistinct; then all four of the dogs galloped out of the darkness and through the front door. More cursing, and a shriek; shots were fired, and some horrible growling. Maya and Jame dashed in and saw that a pair of the dogs had clamped their jaws on the arms of two slovenly men, who were screaming in pain.

Maya stunned the men, being very careful to keep the dogs out of the line of fire.

"How many more?" Maya asked Pax.

"Tree," he said. He pointed at the stairs with his snout. "Uh there."

Three; up there. "Understood," she said. "And the Schanks?"

Pax sniffed the air. He padded into the hallway leading to the back of the house, and stopped at a door, whining.

"Right," said Jame, and set about kicking the door. It was fairly solid, but eventually the door crashed in, revealing a man and a woman, gagged and tied to chairs inside the room. "I'll cut them loose," Jame said. "Can you check what the bastards upstairs are doing?"

"Just a minute," she replied. She adjusted the setting on the energy pistol, setting it higher. "That ought to allow for the thickness of the ceiling here, and the floor up there," she said, and pressed the firing stud.

She was rewarded with two thuds that shook the room. "Must be big fellas," she said.

By then, Jame had freed the Schanks, and the dogs went mad with joy.

Christopher Schank was a small man in his sixties, with grey hair, He looked exhausted. On his right hand was a bloody bandage. Dianne Schank was an attractive women; or would be, after she cleaned herself up. She had curly dark hair shot through with white, and expressive blue eyes.

"Who are you?" she asked as Jame helped her to her feet.

"Maya Komarov and Jame Natwick," she said, holstering her pistol. "Hey, Pax; do you mind going upstairs to check the other two guys?"

The sheepdog barked once, then dashed up to the second floor, accompanied by Willy, a German Shepherd. A few moments later, a shot rang out, and a dog shrieked in pain. Then another scream, but this time it was human.

Maya cursed and ran up the stairs. One of the two robbers had recovered quickly from being stunned, and had shot Willy, who lay in a pool of blood on the floor. Pax had bitten the man, who was on the floor with the sheepdog standing on his chest, growling savagely.

Willy was dead. Pax, Clyde, and Dashiell howled in sorrow.

ONCE THE SCHANKS WERE checked out for injuries, the group returned to their stronghold, rather subdued after Willy's loss. Christopher Schank had had two fingers on his right hand cut off by tinsnips. He was thin and pale, but otherwise was in decent shape. Diane had not been harmed, though they had threatened her. Both man and wife were furious—but at themselves, for not being careful enough as to allow themselves to be kidnapped.

"It's our own fault," Christopher said as they were walking. "We were both outside the compound without our weapons, which is something we have agreed never to do."

"We were lucky this time," Dianne said. She had a husky voice. "I can promise we'll never do that again."

"And because we were so careless, we have lost Willy." Christopher blinked rapidly and wiped his eyes. "He was a good dog."

"We'll have a funeral for him," Dianne said.

Maya suddenly realized that Miron had been rather uncharacteristically quiet for a while. "What's going on?" she asked him.

"Can I have a private word with you?" When she assented, they dropped back, allowing the others to get ahead of them.

"What's on your mind, Miron?"

"Well, I've been thinking. We know the Schanks are doing genetic research... what if I left a copy of Gabriel with them?"

"Hmm. Well, Gabriel is your baby... I guess if you want to do that—and if they have a computer that's suitable—then why not?"

He nodded. "Thanks. I'll discuss it with him when we get back."

She gave him a sideways look. "Do you think he might object?"

"No, not really... it's just that I don't know if he has any opinions about having more than one copy of himself running around."

She shrugged. "If the computer hasn't got any network connections, would it matter?"

"Probably not. Still, he's an intelligent, self-aware entity. I just think it's appropriate to ask him what he thinks of the idea."

Privately, Maya was more concerned with the idea of creating more super-intelligent dogs. She had no moral or ethical objection, but by raising more super-dogs, it was possible that the Schanks might be developing individual beings who might someday decide to supplant them.

She shrugged internally. Ultimately, it wasn't really her concern. "Okay," she said. "See what he thinks about it. I guess it's all right."

Chapter Seven - Unfamiliar Terrain

They escorted the Schanks safely home. Christopher and Dianne were happy to make a gift of their supplies to Maya—which was good, as she said to Jame after they had left the Schanks and were walking back to their camp, "Because I'd hate to have to give all that stuff back. We can sure use it!"

The Schanks were particularly grateful to Miron for sharing an incidence of Gabriel's intelligence matrix with them so that they could continue their research into creating a race of super-intelligent canines even more capable than Pax. Fortunately, their home computer was up to the task of hosting the AI.

Gabriel itself said it was confident that it could help them, always assuming that they could locate and retrieve some sophisticated genetic editing hardware it said they would need to get much further with their work.

Maya was glad they could help Christopher and Dianne, even though she felt a little guilty about holding Pax to his agreement to accompany them to Greensboro. "After having just helped to rescue them from captivity, he should be able to spend time with them," she said to Aiko.

The weapons expert shrugged. "Hey, a deal is a deal," she said.

The Schanks were gracious about it.

"We'll miss him, of course," Dianne said as the island people were packing up prior to departing. "But as long as you can communicate with him easily—"

"*And* as long as you send him home to us once you get where you're going," Christopher said. Putting a hand on his wife's shoulder.

"Well, right—yes," Dianne said. "As long as you do, Maya, we can't object. Pax is his own person. We have raised the dogs to understand that they are not prisoners and that they can leave anytime they like. So far, none has."

"We could not," Pax said, through Gabriel. "This is our home, and you are our family."

In answer, both Christopher and Dianne knelt and put their arms around Pax, who licked their faces, tail wagging. Maya brushed away a tear. *Man,* she thought, *I don't think I have anyone who would cry over me like that.* She glanced at Jame, her lover, but he was watching the little family group and didn't notice.

Presently, having said their goodbyes, Maya, Miron, Aiko, Jame and Carla, with Pax walking beside them, were on their way once more, heading east toward the city that had once been known as Greensboro.

Pax was quiet. Maya knew he was sad about having left his home, and by the death of Willy, so she took it upon herself to spend as much time as possible with the dog. He seemed to appreciate this, and slowly his sorrow drained away. An ebullient creature by nature, he obviously enjoyed being with new friends. And this helped Maya's mood, as well. She liked dogs and had never had the opportunity to really share discussions with one.

Pax, she found, was not learned, despite his intelligence. One night they were sitting side by side, slightly away from the fire, watching the moon rise.

Maya had brought Miron's computer with her. Even though she was getting better at deciphering Pax's speech, she still sometimes found it advisable to have the AI along to interpret.

As the moon slowly appeared over the trees, Pax huffed a little, and then emitted a low whine.

Is he howling at the moon? she wondered. "Do you like the moon, Pax?"

"I have seen it many times in my life," he replied. "I think it is what you humans call beautiful. But it is mysterious."

"Did you know that men walked on it?"

The dog looked at her. "How big is it? I always thought it was small."

She chuckled. "No, it's not as big as the Earth, but it's one of the largest satellites in the Solar System."

"The what?"

"The Solar System. Do you not know what that is?"

"No."

"Oh. Well, you have seen the Moon, and the sun..."

"Yes."

"And of course you know the Earth. The Sun is very far away, ninety-three million miles. It's enormous, it's a huge ball of flaming gas. The Earth and the other planets go around it, like the Moon goes around the Earth."

She went on to explain the Sun's family of worlds, and the moons that circled them. He seemed to grasp the concepts. Then she told him that the stars were also suns, but very far away, and that many of them had their own planets and moons.

"You have seen these other worlds?"

"Well, only as sparks of light." She realized that it would be very hard to explain how exoplanets were found. It would also be very difficult if not impossible to tell him that the stars, including the Sun, were actually as *alive* as he was, and could think and communicate as he could. She drew a schematic of the Solar System in the dirt, explaining the planets to him.

"You can see some of them yourself," she said, looking up at the sky. "For example, that orange one, there; that's Mars. And that very bright one is Jupiter."

He stared at the indicated planets. "Are there people and digs there?"

"Well, there used to be. Men walked on the Moon, and then, later, on Mars. I believe they brought animals with them sometimes."

"This is all new to me," Pax said after a while.

"I used to teach astronomy at the university level," Maya said, "so I can talk about it for hours."

"But where did it all come from? The stars, the Sun, Earth... what made them?"

Sidestepping the issue of divine creation, in which she did not believe anyway, she tried to explain some basic cosmology to him. "Well," she said, "you've hit on some of the biggest questions humanity has even pondered. Where did the universe come from? Where will it end? Let me tell you first off, that we don't really know. As far as we can tell, the universe is about 14 billion years old. We *think* it started off with a vast explosion. Everything in the universe, stars, gas clouds, planets, was originally crammed into a small, hot, dense object called the "cosmic egg." Where *that* came from, we don't know. We *do* know that the universe is expanding. Some people think that the universe will in billions more years begin to pull back into itself, recreating the cosmic egg. And so it would be a cycle of contractions and expansions, like your heartbeat. Other people think the universe is eternal and has always been here."

Pax stared at her. "This makes my head hurt," he said.

She laughed. "A lot of people have that reaction."

The dog was silent for a few minutes. Maya let him grapple with the ideas. She wasn't sure how much imagination and intellectual curiosity he possessed. Such things seemed to be exclusively human concepts. While it was true he had an inquiring nature, that didn't necessarily make him capable of moving out of the physical plane into spiritual concerns. Could he learn to meditate? She doubted it. After a few minutes he said, "If it's true that the stars out there have planets, are there living things on them, as well?"

So he does have a bit of imagination. She smiled ruefully. "Again, all I can say is that no one knows! Before the Dark Years, after the asteroid hit Earth, scientists like me had traveled to the Moon and Mars and had sent robot probes to most of the other planets. None of them found conclusive proof of life. But many scientists are convinced there is alien life elsewhere in space. This was my field of expertise as a teacher, you know: astronomy. I can talk about it for hours."

Once more he was silent. "You know," he said at last, "we dogs are very pragmatic animals. We rely on our eyes, ears, and particularly our noses, to tell us about the world in which we live. We tend to believe only what we can directly experience through our senses. So I can only say that I must believe in the stars and the Moon, because I can see them. But as far as life on other words goes... no, I cannot believe in that. I am willing to consider the possibility, but until or unless I can see, touch, hear, or smell them, I can't believe in aliens."

"Fair enough," Maya replied, hiding a grin. Then she yawned, and said, "I'm done for the night, Pax. Sleep well."

She lay back with her hands behind her head, looking up at the stars. It was warm enough that she didn't feel like sleeping in her tent. Ultrasonic vibrations from a small electronic device kept mosquitoes and other insects away from the camp, so she had no need to be concerned about getting bitten or stung and was able to enjoy the cool night air and the breeze moving through the foliage.

Her conversation with Pax had been interesting, but it served to remind her of the vast, cool intelligences of the stars, far out in the universe. What were they thinking? The islanders had made little progress in capturing their mental emanations or in deciphering the neutrino emissions that was their hallmark.

Pax himself was something of an enigma, as well. The animal clearly possessed human-level intelligence, as proven by his discourse. But, despite the amount of learning overlaying his mind, he was still an animal. *Not that we humans aren't animals,* she said to herself. *But he and his siblings are still driven at least partly by instinct. Will the Schanks succeed in breeding even cleverer dogs? What then? How would they regard Pax?*

She fell asleep with these questions fading in and out of her thoughts.

THE WEATHER WAS MILD for the next few days, and the group made good time on the road. Aiko's leg continued to improve until she was walking as easily as the rest of them. Maya thought hard about revealing the truth about Aiko to Pax but couldn't decide how best to broach the subject. She had already dumped a lot of concept on the dog and wasn't sure that he had the imagination to deal with the reality of the Oracles of Time—or the Rogues, the dark opposites of the Oracles.

She talked to Aiko about it. The Asian woman expressed her own uncertainty. "He is very intelligent," she said, "but you are correct to suspect he may not be capable of freeing his mind from his own essentially physical nature. You humans have evolved in that direction for millennia. Pax, well, he and the other dogs are genetic sports, freaks, if you will. Man-made freaks. Their evolution has been insubstantially different directions, and now here he is with a super-smart brain in a body which is unable to even open a jar. Human beings have a manual dexterity that he simply cannot duplicate. Why, he would need functioning arms, or perhaps tentacles, in order to duplicate what you can do without even thinking. And that would make him a monster."

Reluctantly, Maya had to agree. "So you don't think I should even bring it up."

"That's right. Pax is like an infant in many ways. He is only what, six years old? I know dogs are supposed to age more rapidly than humans, but one reason *homo sapiens* has been so successful on this planet is that you are relatively long-lived. You have been gifted with sufficient time for your brains to mature while you learn about the cultural matrix in which you are embedded." She showed a rare smile. "Your species does quite well, when you are not dropping asteroids on your own heads."

Maya winced. "That's a bit harsh."

Aiko shrugged. "Perhaps. But if you hadn't done that, who can say where your race would be today?"

Then, two days before they reached the outskirts of Greensboro, Maya experienced what she later came to think of as a seizure.

IT HAPPENED WHILE THE travelers had stopped for the night in the crumbling remnants of a church or cathedral. The roof was mostly fallen in, but it still held in a few places, providing decent shelter. After their supper, and a little time spent chatting, the party turned in. As was her habit, Maya lay awake at Jame's side for a while, looking up at the stars. Jame began snoring lightly, and she turned her head to give him a fond look.

It seemed to her that he and she were good together. *Why not continue the relationship?* she asked herself. *There's so much good to be said about him. Handsome, considerate in bed, funny, smart as hell... husband material? Sure—why not?*

Her eyes began closing—and that's when it happened. Later, she characterized the event as a seizure; but, as she admitted to herself, that wasn't really an accurate description of it. Seizures usually caused a disruption of memory and couldn't be recalled. But every aspect of what occurred remained clear in her mind ever after.

She found herself standing in a featureless snowfield that stretched out to the horizon no matter which way she turned. The sky was overcast with an unbroken shield of greyish-white clouds. Directly overhead, a fuzzy patch of light showed where the sun must be.

"So, noonish," she muttered. *Well, once it starts setting, I'll know which way west is. But that won't help me figure out which way I ought to go.*

Or even if I should go anywhere.

Though wearing only a jacket, jeans, and hiking boots—her usual garb following the crash of the aerostat—she wasn't cold, which was a clue that this was a simulation or a hallucination or a dream.

But she couldn't simply stand there, waiting for something to happen, so she picked a direction at random and began trudging through the snow. It didn't seem to be particularly deep. Her feet squeaked in the dry, powdery snow.

Maya recalled that she had been sleeping in their latest camp prior to "waking up" here, but that memory seemed to serve no useful purpose. She kept walking for a long time, suffering no pangs of hunger or thirst. *That's a relief, anyway.*

Eventually she spotted something on the horizon, far ahead. She kept her eyes on it, and it gradually resolved into a tower of some sort. As she drew closer, she saw that it was made of stone blocks, and that there was nothing around or near it: just the stone tower, perhaps thirty feet tall, jutting out of the snowy plain, with some additional snow frosting the crenelations of the tower's top.

"Okay, I'm suitably mystified," Maya said to herself. The closer she got to the tower, the more obvious it became that it had no door, and no other means of entry. There were some arrow-slit windows, but the closest one to the ground was ten or so above her head. She began a slow spiraling circuit of the edifice as she drew nearer.

"Ah ha." There *was* a door: halfway around the base of the thing, hidden from the path of her original approach, was a stout wooden door banded with iron, and a black iron handle to one side.

"Gonna be locked, I bet," she muttered as she crunched up to the portal. She grasped the handle, and sure enough: locked. She sighed.

"Right." She used her fist to bang on the door. "Hey!" she called. "Anybody in there?"

There was no response. Growling a few obscenities, she gave the door a strong kick. To her surprise, it creaked open.

"I've seen this movie," she said, then sighed again. There was nothing for it: she would have to go in.

She peered into the doorway. The interior of the tower was dark, though a little light filtered down through the narrow windows that were evenly spaced along the circular stairway that wound up inside the thing. There was no furniture, and no sign that the tower was tenanted by anyone—or anything. Dust lay thickly on the floor, with no sign that it had been disturbed anytime in the recent past.

Scowling, she began climbing the stairs. About halfway up, she stopped as a voice came to her. It took her a few seconds to realize that the voice was soundless: it was sounding inside her head without having been spoken.

You must not continue into Greensboro, said the voice. It was genderless, as far as she could tell.

"What?" she spat. "What the hell? Who are you? *Where* are you?"

I am in the upper room. You may come up.

"Thanks awfully." Glowering, partly to cover her fear of the unknown, she continued up the steps, around and around the inner circumference of the strange tower.

"What are you doing here? Do you live here?"

I don't live anywhere.

"Kind of what I was afraid of," she murmured. "Listen, my friend, why *shouldn't* I go to Greensboro?"

And at that moment she awoke, to find herself back in her sleeping bag beside the ashes of the campfire they'd built on the floor of the old church. The others in her party stood around her.

"She's awake," Carla said.

"Thank goodness," said Jame, who was crouched down on the floor beside her. "Maya, are you all right? You were crying out in your sleep."

She shook her head to clear the cobwebs of slumber from it. "I was? What was I saying?"

"Something about not going to Greensboro."

She looked blankly at them. "It... it was a dream." But even as she said those words, she knew there was more to her vision than it being merely a dream. There had been the ring of truth to it.

Judging by the sky visible through what was left of the old rafters, dawn was not far off. Maya did her best to describe the dream to her companions, but it was already fading, leaving behind only a certainty that the voice had been delivering a clear warning.

"So, this voice," Jame said, sitting back on his haunches after handing her a cup of coffee. "It was telling you not to go to Greensboro. What about the rest of us?"

"It didn't specify," she replied in a low voice, "but I got the impression that it was just me."

The inhabitants of Eil Malk were not, as a rule, given to superstitions. As an astronomer, Maya was familiar with the history of the science and knew it derived in part from the ancient discipline—if one could call it that—of astrology, which held that the stars could have an effect on the lives of men.

But other supernatural manifestations, such as astral travel, telepathy, and so on, found few adherents among the island's citizens, most of whom prided themselves on their rationality and eschewed pseudoscience. The only reason she knew much about such things was that the old records she had found from the long-dead scientist Santos Dumont, whose work had led her to the truth about the stars, proved that Dumont had been a believer in astrology. He was convinced that the movements of the planets and stars really could provide information human and terrestrial events.

Given the facts about the stars, that they did indeed possess intelligence and could communicate among themselves, Dumont was not completely wrong.

These, however, were things that she had shared with only a few people: Aiko was one.

Now Maya noticed that the Asian woman was gazing at her with intense curiosity. *I think she knows something,* Maya thought. She knew she would have to talk to Aiko soon.

"Just *you?*" Jame scoffed. "What are we supposed to do, *leave* you here while we continue?"

"Um, yes, actually—I think that's exactly what has to happen."

"Well, this is just crazy," Carla said. "We're not going to leave you here."

"I... think you probably should," Maya said, but she was looking straight at Aiko Yokoi as she spoke. Aiko nodded once, very slightly.

Oh, yes, she definitely knows something. "We'll be safe enough here," Maya said. "It's pretty comfortable, and dry. So why not?"

"I will stay with her while you go ahead," Aiko said to Jame. As she spoke, she seemed to swell in size, and Maya had the impression that Aiko was putting a compulsion on their companions. "You *want* to go on."

This suspicion was confirmed when Jame nodded and smiled. "All right, then," he said. Carla and Miron nodded, too.

"We'll go on while you rest, Maya," Miron said. He seemed a little dazed. Jame and Carla also looked glassy-eyed.

"It's fine," Carla said. "We'll take Pax, and he can maybe bring you a message when we arrive. What about it, Pax?"

The dog, Maya was interested to see, appeared to be under the same spell as the humans. Through the AI, he said, "Of course. I will be coming back this way in any case, returning to my home with the Schanks."

"Well, then," Maya said, "that settles it. There's no reason to delay, friends. Aiko and I will be perfectly comfortable here, and you'll be home in a day or so."

"I can't *wait* to see the others," Carla said. They immediately set about packing their camping gear, and within the hour had departed, leaving Aiko and Maya alone.

"So," Maya said after they had gone. "You know something."

"I believe I do," Aiko replied.

"Now you're going to tell me that one of the other Oracles has foreseen some problem in the future and is warning me about it."

"Not... exactly," Aiko said. "Whoever was speaking to you in your dream was likely *not* one of the other Oracles."

"No? Then, who was it? Or was it really just a random dream?"

Aiko was slowly shaking her head. "You have become sensitized enough to the energy levels above the material world for me to say with a fair degree of certainty that it was a legitimate message. Just not from us."

"Then from who?"

"I can't be completely certain, but I suspect—no, I *believe*—that it was one of the Rogues."

Maya blinked at her. "The... the *Rogues*?"

"Yes."

"From one of the rogue *stars*? How in the world can that be possible? Didn't you tell me that they hate planet-based life and want to rid... cleanse the whole galaxy of it?"

"Yes, that's exactly what I told you."

"Then what in the name of the Seven Hathors makes you think that one of *them* would be sending a warning to *us* from space?"

"Because I can't think of where else it could possibly be from," Aiko said. "Believe me, I'm not happy about that deduction, but nothing else makes any sense."

"*That* doesn't make any sense," Maya said. "Why would a rogue star do that in the first place?"

"I don't know. Perhaps... perhaps it has begun to regret its involvement in destroying intelligent civilizations. Perhaps it is in conflict with one of its fellow and is seeking to do it a bad turn."

"I—wow. Look, what are we supposed to *do* about this, anyway?"

"The only thing I can think of, aside from staying isolated by ourselves in order to talk over the situation, is to wait to see what happens."

"That's... not a really good plan, if you don't mind my saying so," Maya replied, with irony.

Aiko folded her arms. "What would *you* suggest, in that case? I'm happy to listen to any ideas you may have."

Maya cast her a sideways glance. Did Aiko sound a little peevish?

For the rest of the day, and the next, the women did little other than make themselves comfortable in their camping area. Aiko took advantage of their solitude by healing herself as quickly as possible, and by sunset of the first day was getting around as easily as Maya. She disappeared for an hour or so and returned with the haunch of a deer for their supper.

Aiko claimed that she had been attempting to contact the other Oracles via telepathy but admitted that something was blocking her efforts. "Probably the Rogues have learned how to screen us out," she said. "Possibly they have even found a way to screen us from each other, which could be why I cannot contact them." She refused to say more on the topic. Maya found this worrisome. It was clear to her that Aiko was perplexed by the thought that the Oracles could be obstructed in any way.

Maya knew enough about them to understand at least something of the Oracles' power. If the Rogues were as powerful as Aiko claimed they could be, Aiko might well have good reason to feel uneasy about not being able to contact her fellows. Maya tried to broach the subject a couple of times, but Aiko remained uncommunicative.

By the end of their second day apart from the others, Maya's frustration had grown until it was annoying her. "I think we should go after them," she said while they were making their evening meal.

"You said that the voice told you not to do that," Aiko pointed out. "Not to go to Greensboro."

"But that's exactly why we ought to go," Maya argued. "If that message was a warning from the one of the Rogues, our friends could be in trouble. Maybe they walked into a trap."

"And we might get into worse trouble if we walk into the same trap."

Maya threw up her hands and said nothing more, but she couldn't stop *thinking* about it.

The next day dawned cloudy and cool, and before they had quite finished breaking their fast, rain began falling. The storm quickly grew worse, until by noon they were forced to stay in the slight shelter provided by the ruins.

Maya had more time to sit and think, and after a while it occurred to her that Aiko seemed to know a lot about the Rogue Stars. Of course, being from the future, such information might have become common knowledge long before her time. Then again...

"Aiko, are you and the other Oracles physical embodiments of stars?"

Startled, the Asian woman stared at her. "What makes you think that?"

"You clearly know a lot about a great many things. You speak authoritatively about the Rogues. I believe you when you say you're from the future—but I can't help thinking there's more to it than that. I think you and the others are more closely associated with the stars than you wish to admit."

Aiko simply stared at her for a long moment, then chuckled. "What an imagination you have," she said.

THE STORM INCREASED in intensity throughout the next couple of hours. Rain pounded on the remaining roof sections of the tumble-down church, and lightning flickered outside, making the few remaining shards of stained-glass sparkle like images in a dream.

Then, around noon, they were startled when someone stumbled into the building.

It was Miron Whitley. He was dripping wet, limping, and bleeding from a bad wound in his left arm. It had been crudely dressed with a piece of torn cloth, but bloody rainwater dripped from it onto the stone floor.

He saw them, gasped, and collapsed.

AROUND SUNSET HE AWOKE. In the interim, Aiko and Maya had stripped off his wet clothing, dried him off, bandaged his arm, and bundled him in their own blankets. The rain had ceased, but the air remained cool and damp. They laid Miron down near the fire to keep him warm and let him sleep.

The first hint Maya had that he had regained consciousness was when he groaned. She crouched next to him and laid a hand across his forehead. "No fever," she said. "So *that's* good. How are you feeling?"

"Terrible. Can I have some water?"

She handed him a cup and he drank greedily.

"What happened?" Aiko asked quietly. "Where are the others?"

"Captured," he said. "Everybody. The others from the *Phoenix*, too." He coughed. "More water?"

Maya fetched more for him. Again he drank, but not as quickly. When he was done, he handed her the cup and said, "Oh, that's good. Thanks."

"So tell us," said Aiko. "What happened?"

"We left here as you know and that first day we made decent time. We pitched camp somewhere outside of Winston Salem, I think. We were so tired from all the walking that I guess we got a little careless. Anyway, Jame was supposed to be standing watch, but he drifted off—and we were ambushed."

"By whom?" Aiko demanded.

"A bunch of armed bandits," he said. "If Jame hadn't fallen asleep... well, there's no help for it. Partly it's my own fault. I should have had Gabriel watch, too. But I was so damn tired that I forgot to set him up, so they caught us." He sighed. "I suppose it's just as well we *were* all sleeping; they might have killed someone if we weren't. As it was, they didn't hurt anybody too badly."

Aiko gestured at his bandaged arm. "Well, how'd you get that, then?"

He touched the bandage. "That happened when I escaped."

"Hey, what about Pax?" Maya asked.

Miron frowned. "I don't know where he is. When the bandits attacked he took off. Smart dog; he knew he'd probably get shot if he tried to help. For all I know, he's hanging around their camp, trying to figure out a way to free our people."

That sounds like something he'd do, Maya thought. Aloud, she said, "And so you got all the way back here on your own?"

"Yeah. I—well, I don't want to get ahead of myself." He went on to explain that the bandits were gun-toting isolationists. "They don't want any contact with anyone, not the tribes in the area, not *any*one. I guess they're sort of like the Bear Clan, because they do kidnap women, but most of the females I saw seemed happy enough. I guess they feel safer with those guys than they do on their own. I mean, who could blame them."

"What did they say when they found out where you and the others were from?"

"Oh, that *really* set them off. They called us foreigners, interlopers, aliens... they kill or enslave people like us."

Aiko scowled. "Did they kill anyone in our group?"

"Well, they had already overrun the Greensboro base. A couple of people there were killed when that happened. Mike Pepper, Dike Ekejiuba..."

"Oh, crap," Maya said in dismay. She had liked both men. Mike had been a computer network technician, and Dike was a medic.

"A couple of others got shot, but not badly enough to die," Miron added.

"We have to rescue them," Maya said. Aiko nodded.

Miron shook his head. "No, you don't get it, Maya. Those bastards are well armed and organized. Like a militia, you know? They have us outnumbered, too. You're not going to just skip in there and straighten everything out."

"Well, then, what?"

"The best we can do is to return to Eil Malk and gather a military force."

Aiko shook her head. Maya said, "That would just take too long. And how are we going to fly the aerostat without a full crew? *I* don't know how to pilot the thing."

"I'm sure I could," Aiko said.

Maya gave her a hard look. But it was probably true, she reflected. The Oracle hiding inside Aiko might well be able to do it. Maya knew that her own mental "conditioning" had made her something of a weapons expert, though she was by no means in Aiko's league. Maya had a good layman's understanding of aeronautical principles, but no hands-on piloting experience whatsoever. And she was not willing to try to learn on the job, as it were. But Aiko... yes, she might be able to successfully fly the *Phoenix*.

Aloud she said, "Be that as it may, I say we've got to rescue them *now*. Somehow. I don't know how."

"I suggest we talk about it on the way," Aiko replied. "We can't stay here, no matter what happens. Miron, will you be able to travel tomorrow?"

"Yes," he said, looking a little grim. "I don't want to lie around waiting for an idea."

They tidied up their camp, packing everything they wouldn't need that night. Then they made dinner and turned in.

Chapter Eight -
Clarity Arises, Twice

They were on the road early the next morning. The humidity was down, and the temperature was fairly cool. Miron insisted that he was perfectly fit to travel, so they kept to a brisk pace.

"What gets me," Maya said, "is how these gangs get women to stick with them. I suppose I'm used to living in an egalitarian society."

Miron scoffed. "That's not what we're dealing with, I don't think. I think life is pretty hard here, without electricity, for the most part, or the other sorts of benefits we take for granted. Good health care, nutrition, education... that stuff doesn't just lie around waiting to be picked up."

"True," Maya said. "And I suppose these men like the idea of having someone pick up after them and take care of their basic needs. The women like being protected, so they gravitate toward the alpha-male type."

Aiko said, "So are you saying that most of the men buying into this lifestyle are insecure types, looking for some woman to prop them up? And the women have been conditioned by culture to take on that job? Those interested in actually living life will live life ignoring this nonsense."

"Well, again, it comes down to options" Miron said. "If your only choice is living with some controlling jerk or starving on your own because you lack survival skills, well, I guess that's an easy choice."

"Unfortunately," Aiko said, "cultures like the ones we're seeing here, with clans and tribes and what-not, base most of their power structure on promoting insecurity and fear. Fear of nonconformity. Fear of the hereafter. Fear of failure. Fear of rejection. If that's taught from infancy, it's hard to liberate those stuck in it. Neither party in that relationship is free, then."

"That sounds about right," Maya said. "So does that make it incumbent on us to change the cultures we find here, assuming we want to move in and colonize these 'lost lands'?"

Miron frowned. "They used to call that sort of thing 'white man's burden,' didn't they?"

"You know your history," Aiko said. "But do you know where the phrase originated?"

"I don't think I do," Miron said after a moment's thought.

"It's from a poem by a forgotten writer named Rudyard Kipling," she replied. "As I understand it, he wrote it to encourage the colonization of the Philippines. It stands as imperialist doctrine, justifying conquest as a way to civilize supposedly 'backward' or 'savage' cultures for their own good."

"Sounds like basically an excuse for a land grab," Maya said.

"Pretty much," Aiko said, and Miron nodded.

"All very interesting," Maya said, "but what we need to do is to come up with a plan to free our friends." As she said these words, Maya was conscious of a new enthusiasm coursing through her being. She hadn't felt this way in a long time. *If I didn't know any better,* she said to herself, *I'd say I've regained some of my passion. All the difficulties we've had... ever since we crashed here, I've been so busy just trying to survive that I didn't notice that I was actually having a good time! Funny how adversity can have beneficial effects, if you just keep an open mind and try to understand the broader canvas. I've learned something about the value of existence.*

The meaning to life.

Who knew?

She walked along with renewed energy in her pace.

Aiko glanced at her. "What are you smiling about?"

"Oh...nothing." But she kept smiling.

Although a specific plan had not yet come clear to her, Maya began to understand that in order to triumph over their as-yet unknown adversaries, the three of them—herself, Aiko, and Miron—would need to use their intelligence along with what they had brought along with them.

They had some weapons, but no doubt they'd be facing superior numbers. What else did that leave that might give them an advantage?

The answer was, their own unique abilities. The only other thing was Gabriel, the artificial intelligence living in the computer Miron carried. Or *had* carried: he hadn't had it on him when he returned.

"I didn't want to be burdened with it," he'd explained, "because I was in such a hurry to get back to you two. Having to carry a computer would have slowed me down too much, especially with an injured arm. Don't worry, I hid it in a safe place, where it can't get rained on and no animals will mess with it. We can pick it up on the way in."

"How did you find your way without a map?" Maya asked.

"Oh, I have a very good memory," he said, grinning. "Come on; you were my professor. You must know that, right?"

"Yeah, I guess that's true," she admitted. "Well, I'm very glad it helped you find us."

Miron was very clever, even if he was injured and not operating at full capacity. But Maya's thinking and memory had been enhanced through her association with the Oracles of Time... and Aiko was an Oracle in disguise, and therefore represented a conduit to the stars themselves.

So, once they acquired Gabriel, how best to exploit these facts?

A day's worth of travel brought no new ideas to her, but she refused to feel discouraged. She was used to trusting her subconscious mind. Often in her life she had found herself worrying about a problem and frustrated that she could not come up with a solution to whatever it might be. At such times, she had gotten used to going for a walk or indulging in some other physical activity in order to give her subconscious time to chew over the problem without her trying to force it to deliver.

On many occasions—in fact, on most of them—by the time she was home again or had finished her walk or workout or whatever other project she was engaged in that was unrelated to the one that was her primary focus, something new had occurred to her; some previously hidden aspect of the conundrum had come to light, and she was able to find a new way to think about it that lead to a solution.

This wasn't something she had told many people. As a university professor she was expected to be quite intelligent, and to have a vast command of facts at her disposal. And, in general, that was true.

But sometimes it wasn't, and this was one of those times. She had no clue how she was going to arrange the rescue of her colleagues.

But eventually she would. She trusted her inner being to provide the answer.

Or at least *an* answer.

Now that Aiko was capable of walking normally, they made good time, even allowing for Miron. Though injured, he was young and strong, and they were able to clean him up and bind his wounds. That night they made camp in the woods to one side of the road, being careful to find a declivity from which their fire would not be visible to any travelers. Miron's face was pale and drawn, but he insisted he was fine—all he needed, he claimed, was a good night's sleep.

The next morning they were all up early, and on their way shortly after dawn.

"We're not too far from Greensboro now," Miron said, consulting Maya's memex, which she had managed to keep in one piece through all their misadventures.

"You said you have such a good memory," Maya said teasingly.

Oh, I do," he said, obviously not taking offense. "But, you know—trust but verify. Anyway, I have a good idea about where we can hole up once we get close and I pick up Gabriel. There used to be a science museum in Greensboro, established way back in the Twentieth Century. It's kind of like the place where we found Yin, remember?"

"That was an amusement park, though."

Miron shrugged. "A museum is a place of amusements, though, right?"

"Do you think we might find another dinobot there?"

"I don't know. Probably not. I wasn't there; I just know about it from looking through old files with Gabriel."

"Hmph."

"I'm pretty sure it's still there; probably in ruins, but hey—we have to take what we can get, eh? Even if it's just bricks and rust, we can use it as a hideout."

Maya looked at Aiko, who shrugged and said, "Okay, it sounds like a plan."

Two more days of travel brought them almost to the outskirts of Greensboro. Miron had been getting stronger, and his color was better.

"We'll be there tomorrow," he said, sinking gratefully to the ground to rest while Maya got a quick meal together.

"That's good, but we need to do some planning first," Aiko said. "If we're outnumbered as badly as you seem to think, then—"

"Please don't move," said a new voice, female and cold. "I would not want anyone to get hurt."

Startled, the three islanders looked up—and saw that they were surrounded by more than a dozen grim-faced women.

Like Blue Petal, the barbarian member of Aly Lynxclaw's tribe of female warriors, these women wore leather armor decorated with metal studs, but in their case the armor was worn over uniforms. The woman who had spoken was taller than the rest, muscular, with a shaved head.

"Neither would we," Maya said quickly. "Listen: do you know Aly Lynxclaw's people?"

A look of surprise flitted across the speaker's face. "What do you know of them?" she demanded, raising her sword.

"Hey, watch it," Maya said, drawing back. "No need for that. We ran into them while we were traveling."

"Explain."

So Maya went over their trials and adventures from the time they had left Eil Malk until they arrived on the lost American continent. By the time she had finished, the tribeswomen had lowered their weapons and relaxed their threatening postures.

"We thought you might have been captive of the man, here," said the leader. The other women murmured assent. "We have had trouble with males in the past. There is a group of them not far from here, nasty people, calling themselves the Black Gang. I'm sure they are the ones who have captured your friends. We've been trying to formulate a way to eliminate them, or at least drive them out of the region." She held out her hand. "I'm Commander Elena Shaw."

"And you know Aly's people."

"We do," Shaw said. "We have traded with them many times. They prefer to live a more primitive type of life than we do. We're more organized."

"I noticed," Maya said dryly.

"To each his own, I always say." Shaw grinned at them. "Come—we'll take you to our compound. You can rest and get cleaned up. I think we may be able to work together to free your friends, and maybe rid this region of those people you call isolationists."

Having little choice, Maya, Aiko and Miron followed Shaw and her people through the woods until they reached what was in essence a walled fortress about two acres in extent, sitting in the middle of a larger clearing. It was well-constructed, with guard towers at each corner of the prison-like compound.

"We don't enjoy living like this," Shaw said as they escorted the islanders through the gate, which rolled back into place after they entered. "But we've been forced into it by the Black Gang. Otherwise we'd live more openly. We had to clear the land all around the walls to prevent them from sneaking up on us.

Shaw's people—mostly women, though there were a few men among them—tended to Miron's injuries while Shaw herself sat in a conference room with Maya and Aiko to discuss the isolationists' plans. Joining them was one of the men, a burly redhead named Josh Bingham.

"Josh went AWOL from the Black Gang," Shaw explained when she introduced him.

Aiko stared narrowly at him. He didn't seem bothered by her scrutiny. "Why did you leave?" she asked.

"I didn't approve of them," he said. He leaned forward and folded his hands on the table. "Look. I grew up around here, in a small village, and it was tough. My father was a hunter, and my mom was a potter. We traded with other villages. Sometimes we didn't have enough to eat, but we always helped each other. We learned to treat other people the way we wanted to be treated."

When he was still a teenager, he said, the Black Gang moved into the area and began raiding the villages for supplies and women. They attacked Josh's village, killing his parents and his older brother, and kidnapping him.

"I was with them for ten years," he said. "All the time, I hated them, but I didn't want to die, so I became one of them." He showed them a circular scar on his right arm. "I was branded. All the men of the Gang are branded. That was Harper's idea."

Maya frowned. "Who's Harper?"

Shaw scowled and spat to one side. "Their leader. A charismatic but ruthless piece of crap. Styles himself a 'general.'"

Maya glanced sidelong at Aiko, who winked at her. Shaw was a self-styled commander. But neither woman said anything.

Josh was still speaking. "That way, if you escape, they can tell who you are if they find you." He shrugged. "And a lot of villages in the area won't take you in, because they're afraid of the Gang. I didn't care, because I knew all along that one day I *would* get away from them. I figured I'd take my chances." He looked at Elena Shaw. "The Gang knew about the Commander's people, here, of course, but they're kind of afraid of them."

Commander Shaw said, "They don't like us. My family were all militia members. Like the Black Gang, I guess, but we were big on defense, and just wanted to be left alone to live our lives. Of course, the Gang can't tolerate that." She smiled. "The biggest problem they have with us was that we were a matriarchy. Still are. But I've studied tactics and strategy, where the Gang relies on strength and numbers. They've attacked us a few times, but we've always managed to beat them back." She shrugged. "I suppose that if they thought they could take us, they'd try it again. But so far, so good. We keep an eye out for them."

Josh raised his hand. Shaw nodded to him. He said, "There's something else. They're always looking for bits and pieces of Old Science."

Miron exchanged glances with Aiko and Maya. "Have they been to the science museum in Greensboro?"

Josh nodded. "Yes, they've scoured the place for anything they could find."

"Okay," Maya said. "We have to assume that they are going to question our friends. That means they're going to find out where we're from."

Shaw looked puzzled. "So where *are* you from?"

Maya explained about Eil Malk, the other islands, and the bionispheres. "We have a pretty high level of technology," she concluded. "And the Black Gang are going to want every bit of it."

"We are so screwed," Miron muttered.

"We have weapons," Shaw said. "Maybe this is the time to really hit those bastards. We can rescue your friends, and get rid of the Gang, all at once." She looked around at the other women, who murmured their assent. So did Josh.

Shaw went on, "We've wanted to hit them, but until now we lacked the manpower and specific intelligence on their operations. If you can help us, it may not matter if we're outnumbered."

"There's something else you should know," Josh said. He gestured at Miron's laptop computer. "They have some of these things."

Maya blinked. "Computers? They do?"

"I don't get it," Miron said. "How is it they even know about computers?"

"I can't answer that, Josh said, folding his arms across his chest, "but I know they do. One of the gang seems to know a lot about them. That's Big Steve. He talked Harper into letting him scour through the ruins of the Science Museum, where he found a lot of old computer parts, and somehow got them all working." He shook his head. "That guy is scary smart. He figured out a way to power the computers using solar cells. Don't ask me how. All I know is, he did it."

"They're more sophisticated than we thought," Aiko said slowly.

"They have the things connected electronically," Josh went on. "They use little cameras and stuff... To keep an eye on the compound's perimeter."

"This puts a whole new complexion on things," Maya said. "We're going to have to take that into account, now, all this computer stuff."

"You know," Miron said, "this might be a good thing for us."

"How so?" Shaw demanded. "None of us knows anything about computers.

"*We* do," Miron said. "I think Gabriel and I might be able to hack into their network. That way, we could supply some real-time intelligence on their movements and defenses."

"You're going to have to explain this to me," Shaw said, sitting back.

They were still discussing strategy when a woman the islanders hadn't seen before burst in. She was black, with cornrows—a hairstyle unfamiliar to Maya and Aiko.

"Commander," she said without preamble. "There's something you need to see."

"All right, Spencer. What is it?"

Spencer ducked out of the room and then came back with another woman, who was accompanied by a sheepdog. Aiko and Maya leaped to their feet. "Pax!" Maya shouted. The dog bounded toward her and jumped up to lick her face.

The militia women looked on in amazement.

"This is *your* dog?" a bemused Shaw asked the islanders.

Pax turned his attention to Aiko while Maya, wiping her face, giggled. It felt great, and she realized that she hadn't laughed in—she couldn't remember how long it had been. She said, "Well, sort of. I mean, he's his own dog, but we helped rescue his owners. His parents. I don't really know what to call them."

It took a while to explain Pax, the Schanks, and their relationship. "So, like I say," Maya said in conclusion, "Pax volunteered to come along with us with the understanding that we'd let him go back to the Schanks after we got safely to Greensboro."

Pax sat at their feet, wagging his tail. Miron had not retrieved Gabriel's computer yet, but he, Aiko and Maya had had enough experience communicating with him to understand most of what he said.

Shaw and the other militia women could not get over their astonishment, but a few simple demonstrations of Pax's intelligence convinced them.

Maya snapped her fingers. "Hey! I have an idea." To Pax, she said, "You know where the Black Gang is holed up, don't you?"

"I do," he said. "I can 'ake you 'ere."

Shaw shook her head. "A talking dog. This is just so crazy."

"But don't you get it?" Maya spread her hands. "Pax can do reconnaissance for us and tell us exactly what they're up to. He can get closer to their hideout than any of us could."

Shaw blinked at her, rubbing her chin thoughtfully. "I... you're right. I bet he could."

"Well, then," said Maya with satisfaction. "Let's put a plan together."

With Pax's input, the islanders and Commander Shaw's people soon devised a plan for a coordinated attack on the Black Gang. After that, while supplies were being gathered, Miron and Pax went to fetch Gabriel from the place where Miron had hidden him. They returned a few hours later with the computer, which was undamaged. Gabriel was indeed able to connect to the Gang's network.

"This is going to be fun," Miron said with glee.

In the meantime, Maya and Aiko, working with the best marksmen among Shaw's people, put together a plan to conduct surveillance on the Black Gang's stronghold.

One important aspect of the surveillance plan revolved around Pax using Maya's memex, which was strapped to his back with its camera pointing out from his side. Pax understood his assignment: he would carry the camera to a vantage point near the Gang's stronghold, from where the camera would supply a video link to the computer housing Gabriel.

"I sure wish we still had Yin," Miron said, staring at the screen.

"We all wish that," Maya said. It was nearly midnight. Josh had told them that the Gang often got drunk at night, leaving only a couple of men to stand guard while the others slept it off.

"That's the best time to attack," Josh said. "The problem is, they *know* they're vulnerable around that time. A head-on assault won't work."

"So, what—are you saying there should be a diversion?" Maya looked at Aiko. "Like what we did when we rescued the Schanks," she said.

Aiko nodded. "I remember."

Josh explained that the only Achilles Heel of the stronghold was a small drainage ditch. "They use it to get rid of waste," he said. "There's a grate where it exits the compound. They know it's a weak point, but to my knowledge, no-one's ever attacked through it. They don't think anyone knows about it."

"They know that *you* do, though," Shaw said. "Don't you think they'll be more on guard?"

"Possibly. But I can't think of any other way to get in. The walls are too strong. You could maybe scale them, but that would probably alert them. Besides, they have dogs."

Maya sucked teeth. "Dogs, eh? Hmmm. Where are they kept?"

Josh drew a crude map of the Gang's compound. "Kennels are here," he said, indicating them.

"Next to the wall," Maya said, studying the map. "Interesting." She got up from the table and went looking for Pax with Miron and Gabriel.

The sheepdog was laying down next to one of the fireplaces in the main building.

Maya explained the plan to him. "It involves a two-pronged attack," she said. "The first part is a diversionary assault on the sewage grating led by Commander Shaw to draw the Gang's forces away from their captives. Do you follow?"

Pax, who was paying close attention to her words, nodded without speaking.

"Good. Now, the other part is a raid led by me, Aiko, and Miron to go over the wall, infiltrate the stronghold and free our companions. You're the most important part of it, Pax; not only for your value in surveillance, but also because you can communicate with the dogs."

"They aren't treated particularly well," Josh had told the planning committee. "It was one of my jobs to care for them. I made friends with them. I like animals."

Through Miron's computer, Pax said, "I'm sure I'll be able to convince the Gang's guard dogs to stand down and allow you and Aiko inside stronghold without attacking you."

Josh had supplied them with a hand-drawn layout of the compound, showing where the island captives were being held. "If you can get in past the dogs," he'd said, "and bring some weapons, your friends will be able to sneak out with you through this side gate. It locks from the inside, so you won't have any trouble getting it open."

"And if anyone tries to follow you out," Shaw said grimly, "we'll handle them."

Pax was sure the Gang's dogs wouldn't cause any trouble. He would lead them out, too, he said.

Shaw had accepted the sheepdog as an equal in the escape plan. "If you can do that," Shaw said to Pax, "we'll welcome the dogs in and treat them well."

"I'd be happy to care for them" Josh said. "I think they'll be lots better off here than with the Black Gang."

"I like this plan," Maya said, and Aiko agreed.

"And I can keep the Gang's network from alerting them to any incursion," Miron said.

Two nights later they were ready. Shaw and ten of her most skilled warriors accompanied Maya, Aiko, Miron and Pax through the woods toward the Black Gang's compound. Maya's memex, which was set to camera mode, was strapped to Pax's back with a harness made by one of Shaw's women, a skilled leather craftsperson.

Moving as soundlessly as possible, the rescue party moved into position around the wall surrounding the Black Gang's redoubt. Maya found herself agreeing with something Shaw had said: the wall was something of a tactical mistake, because the Gang never patrolled outside it, feeling confident that anyone who got inside would be speedily incapacitated by the dogs.

"They have put a lot of faith in their silly little computer network," Miron said scornfully. "They simply never expected anyone else in the region to be computer savvy." He tapped away at the computer's keyboard. "Okay," he said with satisfaction. "None of their alarms are going to sound now. It's time to get things started."

Shaw's people quietly boosted Pax up to the wall. The dog had a rope tied to the harness with a slip knot. Shaw herself had the other end of the rope and lowered him gently to the ground inside. The knot came loose, and Pax took off into the dark.

Via the camera, which was broadcasting to Miron's computer, they watched as Pax encountered one of the Gang's dogs, a Great Dane. Everyone tensed, because the dog barked a few times—then stopped, as it listened to Pax. Evidently the sheepdog was able to win the Great Dane over, because it stopped barking, cocked its head to one side, and woofed softly a couple of times. The two dogs then walked together farther into the compound.

Having achieved the first of the goals, Shaw gave the go-ahead signal to the team waiting at the drainage grate. Using bolt cutters, this team chopped through the grate and ducked into the drain pipe.

Shaw turned to Maya and grinned. "So far, so good. Our turn."

The plan called for them to rappel over the wall once the dogs, under Pax's direction, began a mock fight, barking and snarling as savagely as possible to attract the attention of the gang members, many of whom would be asleep.

"They think the alarm system will wake them up if anyone tries to get in," Josh said. "They never thought anyone could ruin that for them."

Moments later, the dogs began fighting. It sounded terribly vicious, with ferocious growling. "Go!" Shaw snapped as soon as the sound reached their ears. Using a weighted throw line with a hook secured to the end, she tossed her rope over the wall. It caught, and she swarmed up it. Maya did the same, but it took her three tries to get a secure hold. By that time, the other raiders were already trotting through the compound, unmolested by the dogs—who were putting up a hell of a fight near the main gate, as far from the drainage ditch as possible.

Maya and Aiko were spearheading the rescue attempt, backed up by Shaw and her warriors. Following memorized instructions, they headed straight for the house. Lights were already coming on inside.

Maya drew her energy gun. Its charge was way down, but she knew she still had enough left to stun five or six antagonists. Once the gun was emptied, she'd have to rely on hand-to-hand fighting. Fortunately, martial arts had been part of her training. She was actually hoping to tackle someone, to wreak a little vengeance for what had been done to her friends.

It was almost ridiculously easy to infiltrate the house. Two men dashed out the door; she dropped them both with her gun, then ducked in, followed by Aiko.

Three more men and a woman confronted them, but Aiko took them all out.

"Down there," Maya said, pointing at a hallway leading off to one side. "They should be in the third room to the left."

She stood guard outside the room while Aiko tried the handle. It was locked—but the Asian woman reared back and kicked the door, hard. It took her three tries, but on the third the door flew open, hanging by one hinge.

"Well," she said, turning to Maya. "That wasn't so hard, was—" There was the report of a gun, and blood splashed from her head. She collapsed, shot in the face.

"Aiko!" Maya dropped into a crouch. Another shot slammed into the wall behind her. She cursed and fanned the room with the last of the charge from her gun. Several thuds told her that everyone in the room was down.

That included the two hostages, she saw as she peered cautiously around the corner of the door. Jame and Carla were slumped in chairs, to which they had been tied.

Laying on the floor in front of them, facing the doorway, was a big, bearded man with a shaved head. From descriptions she had been given, she knew this was "General" Coleman Harper.

Working swiftly, Maya removed his belt and secured his hands. The stun effect would wear off within moments. Once he was immobilized, she turned her attention to Aiko. The wound was terrible, but Aiko was still breathing.

"Come on, come on," Maya moaned. She knew that the Oracle wasn't really human, that Aiko was merely a form she had adopted—but she did not know whether or not Aiko could be killed, or if she could heal herself after having sustained such a terrible injury.

So consumed with concern was she that the sound of a throat being cleared startled her. She turned her head and saw Harper, awake and grinning at her.

Her eyes narrowed as she advanced on him, furious, ready to pistol-whip him with her gun.

"Nice work," he said, managing to make it sound like a taunt. "I didn't really think anyone could get in here."

"I had help," she snapped. "Give me one good reason why I shouldn't kill you, Harper."

"I can't, really," he said. "I certainly would kill me, if I were you."

"Not a good argument," she said through gritted teeth.

He scoffed. "People like you, you're weak," he said.

She put a foot up on the chair, between his legs, and leaned over. "I see," she said. "And people like you, you're pretty damn stupid, mocking someone holding a gun on you."

Her eyes cut toward Aiko, who was gurgling from the blood running into her mouth.

At that moment, Carla coughed. Her eyes fluttered open and focused on her. "Oh, hey," she said, straining against the ropes binding her. "Cut me loose, would you?"

"Sure." She took out her knife and cut the ropes. "Are you okay?"

"Yeah."

"Good. See if you can do anything for Aiko. This piece of garbage shot her."

Carla exclaimed, then dashed over to where Aiko lay.

Now Jame started coming round. He coughed and spat.

"Hon!" Maya said. "Are you all right?"

"Pretty much," Jame said. He had a black eye. "Had a bit of a tussle with one of these morons. Not this one," he added, rubbing his wrists and pointing at Harper with his chin. "But here's some news. You know how we've been wondering if there's anyone left alive on the Moon, after all this time? The General, here, has been in contact with them. They've been feeding him notes on Old Science technology. It's a good thing you came when you did, because they were just about ready to set up an electronic guard system for this place."

"Oh?" Maya turned to Harper. "In return for what?" She was beginning to feel overwhelmed. The raid, the Gang, Aiko being shot, and now an alliance between the Gang and the Moon-dwellers. It was a lot to take in.

Harper scowled and remained silent.

Jame said, "I can tell you that. He's been trading information on Earth's resources."

"Well, now," Maya said. Following Aiko's death, her anger had been simmering and now threatened to boil over. "How much, exactly, do you even *know* about Earth's resources? Living like you do, holed up in your little den here in the middle of North Carolina." She scoffed. "Seen a lot of the world, have you?"

He sneered. "We have means," he said.

She slapped him, hard. He glared at her.

Pax padded into the room. "All glear," he said.

"Thanks," she said. "Jame, can you free our friends?"

"Glad to!" He hurried out of the room.

Harper's eyes had gone wide. "Did that animal just *speak*?"

"He did. Maybe there are still some things going on around here you're not aware of. Pax here convinced your dogs to help us."

Harper drew a breath. "Well, it won't matter, in the end. The Loonies will help us. Enjoy your little triumph while you can."

"Correct me if I'm wrong," Maya said dryly, "but how are people who are used to gravity one-sixth that of Earth going to manage here? Because, if they've been living on the Moon for the last few hundred years, unless they're doing a tremendous amount of exercise, they are going to be moving like they're weighted down with lead if they land."

"Maya!" Carla called out from where she was crouching beside Aiko.

"Yeah?"

"She needs medical attention fast."

"Hmm." Maya turned to Harper. "Where's your first aid stuff?"

Harper said nothing.

Maya nodded. Okay." She lifted his bound hands and bent the little finger on his left hand back until it snapped.

He grunted but did not cry out.

"Tough guy," Maya said thoughtfully. She broke the little finger on his right hand. "I can keep doing this until we run out of fingers," she said mildly. "Then we can start in on... other things."

Harper was pale and sweating. "Okay, okay," he said. "In the hall, two doors down on the left."

Carla raced out of the room and returned moments later with a bundle of medical supplies.

"None of this will do you any good," Harper said. He was still sweating, and in obvious pain. "They know where we are. They'll be coming."

"Mmm. See my above remarks about gravity."

"Won't matter. They're already here, on Earth. They know what you're doing."

"Do they, now?"

Aiko murmured something.

"What did she say?" Maya demanded.

Carla said, "I dunno. Sounded like 'Get Royce.'"

Maya turned to Harper. "That one of your men?"

He scowled at her. When she reached out for one of his injured hands, he said, "Yeah, yeah. Carl Royce."

Jame came back into the room, leading the rest of the Greensboro team, fifteen people in all. They immediately began praising Maya and the others.

"Not now, folks," she said. "Who here knows Carl Royce? One of the Gang."

"I do," said one of the women. "He's some sort of computer specialist. We didn't even know they had computers. Want me to find him?"

"Please. It's safe out there; we have all these losers rounded up. Jame? Can you go with her, please?"

The woman nodded and hurried out. Jame, casting a puzzled look at Maya, followed her.

One of the other Greensboro team said, "Maya, it's great to see you, but these idiots have been in touch with people on the Moon. They're—"

"We know. Dealing with it."

A few minutes later, the woman, a botanist named Sherry Dorin, returned with a rather battered-looking man, hands bound, in tow. He was being urged along by Jame.

Carla said, "Aiko wants you to bring him to her. Maya, she's dying."

"I know. What does she want with this fool?"

As soon as Royce caught a glimpse of Aiko, he recoiled, and began twisting and turning, trying to get away. Jame cuffed him. "Knock it off," he growled.

"Maya!" Carla called. "She's having a seizure!"

Maya, shocked, looked on as Aiko began thrashing about on the floor. At the same time, Royce fell to his knees, shivering and quaking.

"What the hell is going on?" Jame demanded.

Aiko's body convulsed one final time and began *dissolving*. No one could move: they stared as her dwindling form released clouds of vapor into the air.

"She's... sublimating," Jame whispered, rapt. "Like... like dry ice."

Royce likewise began convulsing. His flesh ran like liquid wax, his features seeming to refashion themselves. His body, too, emitted a thick fog, all but hiding him from view.

Moments later the fizzing and hissing died away, and Aiko lay on the floor in place of Royce, her small form swimming in the large man's clothing.

Before anyone could speak, Aiko's eyes opened. She smiled, and said, "Hellay. Oh, I see our friends are back," she added, spotting the Greensboro people.

"What just happened?" Maya whispered.

Aiko smiled gently. "It's easy enough to explain," she said, rising from the floor. "Wow. That was some transition!" She giggled. "I know, you're all really confused." She sighed. "Well, it's as I thought: the Rogue Stars have got a foothold in this Solar System."

The Greensboro contingent looked at each other. "What in the world?" Sherry Dorin said. "What are you talking about?"

"We'll have to explain later," Maya said. "But okay, for now, Aiko—I follow you. The Rogues. They're here. Like... like the Oracles are here?"

"Yes, exactly like that. As I had suspected. And this person, Royce—he was one." She gestured at herself. "Like me. A, a projection,

I guess you could say. Fortunately, I was able to override his masquerade and push him out. Then I took over his body, because mine was so badly damaged. I was losing control and had to make the move before I was forced to discorporate."

"I am completely at sea here," Miron murmured.

"Like she said, it's going to take some explaining," Maya said. "But I know what she's talking about."

"And now," the new Aiko said, "Miron: check with Gabriel. Harper's right, you know; They're coming. They've dispatched a fleet of drones to overwhelm us and take control back."

Chapter Nine - Predetermined Destiny?

"**D**amn!" Maya turned to Miron. "Is there anything you can *do* about this?" Again, she felt overwhelmed: things were happening so quickly that she had barely enough time to accept Aiko's bizarre transformation—but there was no time to think about that now.

"Um, I..." Miron swallowed hard. "Just a minute." He tapped frantically at the keyboard. Then he went pale and looked up at his companions. "They'll be here in fifteen minutes. There is one thing that might work," he said. "But—"

"But me no buts, Miron," Maya barked. "Whatever it is, do it!"

"All right." He sucked in a deep breath. "The drones are being controlled from orbit."

"What?" Maya demanded.

"Yes. Gabriel has traced the signal. The Moon Dwellers must have inserted a satellite into orbit... I don't know how they got the capability, but they did. I think I can jam the broadcast using the equipment here."

"You're not going to have time to do that," Jame said. He was sweating.

"Normally, that would be true," Miron told him. "But Gabriel says he can upload himself into their network sort of like a computer virus, and overload it, wiping its memory."

Maya frowned. "Wait—what will happen to *him*?"

"It will wipe me from the network's memory, as well," Gabriel said over his external speakers. "But Miron can recode me when you get back to Eil Malk. This is the only way. Its own defensives will block me unless I keep it so busy that it will not have time to do that."

Maya didn't hesitate. "Gabriel, thank you. We'll never forget this." She nodded to Miron. "Do it, if you're sure it'll work."

"As sure as I can be," he said grimly, and started typing.

Carla, who had been peering out the window. Outside, dawn was breaking. "Here they come!"

Maya dashed to the window. A swarm of black dots had appeared in the south, growing larger as they came closer to the Gang's hideout.

"If you're gonna do this, you better do it now," Maya said to Miron.

"Just another few... ah. Here we go." He hit the ENTER key.

In the sky, the drones began exploding.

THREE WEEKS LATER, back on Eil Malk, Maya was sitting in her old office in the university campus, surrounded by familiar books and the usual untidy mess of papers. She felt very comfortable there.

The expedition to open up the lost continent of North America had been a qualified success. A beachhead had been established. Jame and Miron were still there; Maya would join them in a few months.

It had been difficult to convince the island's government that the Oracles even existed, let alone the Rogue stars. The knowledge upended everything the establishment knew—or thought they knew—about the universe, Old Science, and the people living on the Moon. But now everyone was aware of the dangers posed by the Rogues, and even the Moon colony's legitimate government had at last agreed, albeit somewhat unwillingly, to open communication with the mother planet. As Maya had said, "We can't afford to ignore each other any longer. We have to work together. The stars can be ours, if we do."

All the bionispheres in the island group had agreed to join a confederation in order to protect themselves against future attacks by the Rogues and their allies.

Maya had become more relaxed, and surer of herself. Life had a renewed meaning for her. A lot of work remained to be done, but her belief in the power of unity and knowledge convinced her that nothing was impossible.

Jame had proposed, and she had accepted.

She now understood the meaning of life. It was not just about her; It was about helping others like Blue Petal, the Shancks, the bionipheres, and friends like Pax. And having a fun time along the way, on the journey of life. By being present, and not getting so caught up in the challenges of life.

Now she sat looking out her office window at the hustle and bustle of daytime traffic through the bionisphere's streets. Outside in the hallway she heard the voices of students. Soon it would be time for her to go to the lecture hall for her class.

Life, she decided, was good.

Don't miss out!

Visit the website below and you can sign up to receive emails whenever WAI CHAN publishes a new book. There's no charge and no obligation.

https://books2read.com/r/B-A-IHWU-UHQAF

BOOKS 2 READ

Connecting independent readers to independent writers.

www.ingramcontent.com/pod-product-compliance
Lightning Source LLC
Chambersburg PA
CBHW052006170626
46808CB00007B/2803